The Best of Erotica

SELECTED BY MAXIM AND DOLORES JAKUBOWSKI

NEON

A NEON PAPERBACK

This paperback edition published in 2006 by Neon
The Orion Publishing Group Ltd.
Orion House, 5 Upper Saint Martin's Lane
London WC2H 9EA

A CIP catalogue record for this book is available from the British Library.

Printed and bound in Great Britain by Mackays of Chatham.

ISBN 1-905619-02-2

Contents

The Restaurant

J.P. Kansas

The limousine took Melissa and Harold, her fiancé, to a part of the city she had never seen. Harold had been quite mysterious about their destination and the purpose of the trip. It was a game he often liked to play. Melissa enjoyed indulging him, but she also liked to pretend that his surprises never impressed her.

In the middle of an otherwise dark and apparently deserted block stood an elegant brownstone, its entrance marked by a well-lit awning and guarded by a doorman in full livery. The doors were deeply stained mahogany, with frosted glass windows elaborately carved in a floral pattern.

The doorman opened the doors for them and they stepped into a small entrance foyer. Harold opened the inner door and Melissa stepped inside.

She found herself in what appeared to be an elegant restaurant decorated in the Victorian manner. "This is not too unattractive," she conceded. "I told you," Harold chided her, leading her by the elbow toward the tuxedo'd *maitre d'*.

As Harold had requested, Melissa was wearing a black silk dress that buttoned all the way up the front. He had told her she looked especially beautiful in it. Harold was wearing one of his most conservative suits. He looked quite handsome.

"Do you have reservations?" asked the *maitre d'*, acting as if he didn't recognise Harold, who, she gathered, had been there several times before.

"Yes, we do," Harold replied. "The name is Smith."

She was a bit surprised — Smith was not Harold's last name. Harold smiled at her and gave her a wink, a gesture she had rarely seen him make.

The *maitre d'* consulted the absurdly large leather reservations book at his side and ran his long, manicured finger down the list. "Ah, yes, for two at eight o'clock," he said, tapping the entry. He turned. "If you'll follow me, please," he said, walking briskly down the centre aisle. They followed him.

The room was panelled in dark wood. Brass sconces cast a diffused light. Exquisite flower arrangements were displayed in delicate Oriental vases. Melissa could smell their delicious perfume. The floor was lushly carpeted. Somewhere a harpsichord was playing.

On each side of the aisle was a series of recesses, the entrances draped with thick, heavy curtains. One could hear sounds from within, but they were muffled and indistinct. Melissa got a glimpse of one of the patrons as a waiter came out of one of the alcoves, but she could not tell what she had seen.

The *maitre d'* stopped halfway down the aisle and opened a set of curtains on the left. "In here," he said.

They stepped into the recess. It was about eight feet by six feet, with a built-in banquette on three sides upholstered in a purple, velvety fabric. The seat facing them was loosely draped with several pieces of dark cloth.

Running above and behind the banquette was a shelf holding more flower arrangements. On the carpeted floor were several footstools, upholstered in the same fabric as the banquettes.

There was a small door on one side of the curtained entrance and a coat stand on the other.

Harold removed his coat jacket and hung it on the tree. He and Melissa sat down side by side on the banquette. The velvet was thick and pleasing to the touch. "Your waiter will be here in a moment," the *maitre d'* murmured, and let the curtains fall as he backed away.

"Where are the tables?" she asked. Despite herself, she was puzzled and curious.

"We're not dining now," Harold told her, taking her hand.

Melissa realised that the night's entertainments would be sexual. She should have guessed earlier: many of Harold's surprises involved sex in one way or another. He particularly enjoyed finding establishments that offered erotic performances, where she would often be the only woman in the audience.

Although he was older than she was, he seemed to her in many ways like a child, often behaving as if he believed that sex was something he himself had discovered or invented. He preferred to believe, Melissa thought, that she had been a virgin when they met, although they had both been married and divorced. It was one of the many things they never talked about.

"I promise that you'll enjoy it," he said, turning to her with his handsome, powerful eyes. He kissed her on the lips and she softened against him, letting him enter her mouth with his tongue. "I love you so much," he murmured as their lips parted.

They sat without speaking for a few moments. The curtains opened and a young woman entered the recess, letting the curtains fall closed behind her. She was young and attractive, with long, blonde hair that fell in ringlets around her face. She wore a simple white blouse and black skirt, and she carried two large leather folders. “Good evening, sir. Evening, ma’am. Would you like to see the menu, or do you know what you’d like tonight?”

“Let me take a look at the menu,” Harold said.

Melissa did not want to spoil Harold’s surprise. “You can order for me,” she told him. The woman handed Harold the menu and he opened it. “Shall I give you a few minutes, sir?” she asked him.

“That won’t be necessary,” he said, barely glancing at it. Melissa suspected that he had already given a lot of thought to his selections. “For the appetiser, we’ll both have number three. For the main course, I’ll have eleven and the lady will have nine.”

“Very good, sir,” she said, accepting the menu from Harold again. “And wine?”

He waved his hand. “Your house Bordeaux. A carafe.”

“Very good, sir.” A few moments later a young man appeared, carrying a tray with the carafe of wine and two glasses. Like the young woman he was blonde and attractive, wearing a white shirt and black pants. He set the tray down on the shelf behind the banquette to their right.

“Shall I pour, sir?”

“Please.”

He filled the glasses and handed them to Harold and Melissa. Harold waited for him to leave, and then lifted his glass to her. The glass was hand-blown and expensive. “I’ve dreamed of this for months,” he whispered. His eyes were dark and wide with excitement. “To our love.” He emptied his glass. She smiled at his boyish romanticism. “To our love,” she echoed, and took a small taste. It was surprisingly good for a house wine.

"Drink it down, my sweet," he urged her. She finished her glass, and Harold refilled both glasses. This time he let her sip it slowly.

The curtains parted again and this time two young women entered, dressed in the same way as the others. Like them, they were blonde, and they were both very lovely. Their hair was pinned up. The one facing Melissa had small blue eyes and a lush mouth. The woman opposite Harold had huge brown eyes and a small cupid's-bow mouth. They kept their eyes downcast as they each brought a footstool and placed them directly in front of Melissa and Harold, and then kneeled before them.

The young woman in front of Melissa lifted her hands to the hem of her dress. Melissa turned her head to look quizzically at Harold. None of his surprises had ever involved someone else actually touching her.

He squeezed her hand reassuringly, but said nothing.

The woman unbuttoned Melissa's dress all the way to the neckline, parting it to reveal the flowered silk slip underneath.

The woman at Harold's feet unfastened his belt and unzipped his trousers. As he raised his hips slightly, she grasped the waistband and the elastic of his underpants and brought them both down to his ankles in one smooth gesture. He was still covered, however, by the long tails of his dress shirt.

Melissa's attendant brought her hands down to the hem of the slip and gathered it up Melissa's thighs.

"Lift your hips," Harold whispered to Melissa, giving her hand a squeeze. "You must help her."

Melissa sighed. She had not been touched sexually by another woman since college — it seemed such a long time ago. She looked down at the attendant. She could not see the woman's face clearly, but she seemed so serious, so completely absorbed by her task.

Melissa lifted her hips, and her attendant raised the slip up past her waist to uncover a new pair of beautiful silk panties.

Melissa was so interested in watching her attendant that she was barely aware of Harold's who had been unbuttoning his shirt and parting its tails. Melissa found it strange and exciting to see his erect penis in these circumstances. It was like a little soldier at attention, quivering slightly with every pulse, its mouth already gaping.

Melissa's attendant reached to the waistband of her panties and gave them a slight tug. It was an absurd situation — but it was so terribly arousing. Melissa lifted her hips and let the attendant slip them down.

Melissa wondered how long Harold had been planning to take her there. How many times he had come here by himself or with other men? She knew that Harold was a man of the world and had the money and inclination to indulge himself. But it seemed so...she fumbled for the right word... overelaborate.

And yet — and yet the situation was ridiculously, deliciously exciting. She was already wet inside, and her clitoris was throbbing like a tiny drum.

The attendants each opened another drawer in the base of the banquette and brought out a pair of thin latex gloves like the ones physicians wear. As they put them on, Melissa trembled in anticipation.

As Harold's attendant reached for his penis with both gloved hands, Melissa's attendant grasped her thighs just above the knee, pulling them forward and apart. Melissa's right knee came to rest against Harold's left. She leaned back against the seat and her hips rolled backwards. She felt her labia separate and open.

Her attendant moved her hands up Melissa's thighs to the crotch, and she gasped with pleasure. The latex of the gloves was barely perceptible, making the attendant's skin flawlessly smooth and dry. The woman's touch was light but full of self-assurance. She caressed Melissa, running the heel of one hand over Melissa's clitoris as she petted the labia with the fingers of her other hand.

Melissa looked over to see what Harold's attendant was doing to him. She was surprised to discover that she did not feel jealous or angry to see another woman's hands caressing his penis — in fact, she found it fascinating. His attendant was remarkably imaginative, and Harold seemed to he lost in the pleasure of it.

Melissa's attendant was doing remarkable things to her, too. Like most people, when Melissa masturbated, no matter how long she wished to prolong the pleasure and no matter how inventive she wished to be, she found her hands inevitably performing a repetitive and persistent movement that equally inevitably would lead to orgasm. But her attendant was doing no such thing. She was caressing Melissa as if without any goal at all, but simply for the delight of touching her. And, although the attendant was of course touching the same spots again and again, it was without any pattern or regularity.

Remarkably, Melissa didn't find it at all frustrating, as when an inept lover fumbled ignorantly, nor did she have the feeling she was being teased. No; she was endlessly surprised and delighted and ever more and more aroused, but with no sense of impending orgasm – and no sense that her pleasure would ever end.

Melissa closed her eyes and sighed again and again, and the delicious fragrance of her arousal mixed with the perfume of the flowers in the vases. She opened her eyes. She looked down at Harold's penis in his attendant's hands, and saw that its mouth was now filled with clear fluid.

As if taking this as a signal, his attendant went again to the drawer and took out a small foil packet. Opening it, she removed a condom, and Melissa watched in fascination as the attendant rolled it down onto Harold's penis. It was the thinnest Melissa had ever seen, and completely transparent. If she hadn't just seen the woman put it on him, she would never have known he was wearing one.

Melissa's attendant took her hands away, reached into a drawer, and removed another foil packet. She opened it and took out what appeared to be a piece of the same material as Harold's condom: transparent, and quite thin and flexible. She fitted it between Melissa's legs, from above her pubic hair down between her cheeks. It felt as light as a spider's web. The attendant smoothed it out, pressing against Melissa's thighs, from the tops down to the buttocks. There were two adhesive strips to keep the material in place, but Melissa could barely feel them.

Now both attendants moved even closer. Harold's attendant moved her mouth to his penis and Melissa's attendant brought her mouth to Melissa's vulva.

Melissa and Harold both sighed at the same time as their attendants touched them. They were still holding hands, and Melissa squeezed Harold's hand to let him know how much pleasure she was feeling. She was surprised at how wet and slick her attendant's tongue felt. It was as if there was no difference between the woman's mouth and her own flesh.

She closed her eyes with the pleasure of it, and let her head fall against Harold's shoulder. No one – not Harold, not her first husband, not any of the lovers in between, none of her boyfriends in college, not even the roommates she had experimented with — had ever used mouth and tongue and fingers on her as this woman was doing.

Like the caresses of her hands, the attentions the attendant bestowed were continually surprising, endlessly inventive, without repetition, and always arousing. She did things Melissa had never felt before, and never imagined. The attendant turned her head slightly and sucked the flesh of Melissa's outer labia into her mouth; holding it gently between her teeth, she rolled her tongue back and forth along it. She took Melissa's clitoris into her pursed lips and then blew on it, as if to inflate it. Through the thin, strong film, she probed Melissa's anus with her tongue. And, all the while, her fingers caressed and stroked everywhere her lips and tongue were not.

Melissa heard someone moaning softly again and again, and opened her eyes to realise that it was herself. The pleasure of the woman's attentions had permeated her body like a warm fluid, and her orgasm was as inevitable as a thunderstorm when the clouds gather.

Harold, too, was moaning quietly, and Melissa turned slightly to see what his attendant was doing. Harold's attendant had her head tilted to one side, and was sucking on the underside of his penis just below the glans. One hand held the shaft, just below her mouth, and the other hand cupped his scrotum.

As Melissa watched, Harold's attendant started to shift position, but with his free hand he reached for her head and moved it back again.

The attendant returned her lips to their previous position on his penis and did something with her hands. Abruptly, Harold groaned and shifted his pelvis forward. Melissa watched the first burst of semen fill the small pouch at the tip of his condom. Even as the second spasm took place, Harold was turning to Melissa, kissing her, filling her mouth with his tongue.

Melissa's attendant sucked her clitoris between her lips and trilled her tongue against it, and Melissa drowned in an endless cloudburst of pleasure.

They came to themselves gradually. Melissa settled back against the cushions of the banquette. Harold's attendant carefully removed his condom, tied it closed, and shut it away in another drawer in the banquette.

Melissa's attendant removed the transparent film, painlessly peeling the adhesive strips from Melissa's skin, and discarded it. Each attendant produced a moist disposable cloth like the kind used to clean infants and gently swabbed both of them off, then used soft cloths to dry them. Finally, the attendants removed their surgical gloves and discarded them.

"I understand you're both having a main course, sir," said Harold's attendant. Her voice was soft and sweet.

"Yes, we are," Harold replied.

"Are you ready for them now, or would you like a few more minutes?"

Again Harold looked at Melissa inquiringly. "I'm ready," she said.

"Now will be fine," Harold said.

"Then, if that will be all, sir. I hope everything was to your pleasure, sir?"

"Yes, it was."

"Ma'am?" Melissa's attendant asked softly, her eyes still downcast.

"Yes, thank you."

"Thank you, ma'am."

The two women stood up, continuing to keep their eyes down. If they had been at all moved by the experience, they gave no signs of it. They backed away and disappeared through the curtains.

Melissa and Harold were alone again. She sensed that Harold was waiting for her to speak. "I'll have some more wine, please," she said. He refilled their glasses and handed hers to her.

She drank most of her glass. "What I wonder is, will you have enough appetite for the main course, whatever that may be?" She didn't remember Harold ever having such an appetite when it was the two of them alone together. Of course, she had no idea what he did before he was with her, or after.

"I'll be fine," he replied, and drained his glass. "Everything is so well done here, I find that it's never a problem."

She wanted to ask him how much their evening was costing, but money was another of the many things they never discussed.

"Shall I remove my dress while we're waiting?" she suggested. "It's already getting creased."

"That might be a good idea."

Still sitting, she stepped out of her panties, and then stood up and removed her dress. She hung both next to Harold's jacket. "I think I'll just leave the slip on," she said, straightening it down as she returned to the banquette.

"I'm sure that will be fine."

After a minute or two, the curtains opened again, and Melissa was astonished to see two young men, dressed like all the others, step into their cubicle. She turned once again to look at Harold, but he only smiled and winked at her. He had never once given the slightest hint of such an inclination.

The two men were quite handsome. The one standing before Melissa had dark hair, a long Roman nose and a strong jaw. The one in front of Harold was rather delicate, fair-skinned, with curly blonde hair.

Almost immediately they undressed, slowly and deliberately, hanging their clothing on the coat stand in the corner. Harold had taken her to several establishments where male dancers undressed for the enjoyment of an audience of women — Harold often had to bribe someone to be allowed in with her — but these young men were not trying to make an entertainment of it. Still, Melissa was fascinated, and found herself becoming excited again.

The recess was small, and they were standing quite close. Melissa's man had a well muscled body with a long, uncircumcised penis. Harold's was fit, but seemed a little softer, his muscles less prominent. His penis was slightly smaller than the other man's, and circumcised. Neither was erect, but Melissa noticed that Harold's was already stirring.

The two attendants knelt before them as the women had done, opened drawers in the banquette, put on thin latex gloves, and removed foil packets. The man in front of Melissa opened the packet and then, rising up on his knees, offered her the condom. She hesitated only a moment before taking it.

To her right, Harold's attendant had done the same thing. Harold was already unrolling the condom on to his attendant's penis, which was rapidly engorging. Melissa found the sight of her fiancé's hands on another man disturbing and arousing. Using both hands, she unrolled the thin, almost invisible material over her attendant's penis.

Harold stroked his man's penis with both hands until it became fully erect. Almost without realising it, Melissa was mimicking his actions with her own hands. Her attendant's penis grew large and erect.

Harold leaned forward and took his attendant's penis into his mouth. Melissa could scarcely believe what she was seeing, and her entire body seemed to flush with excitement.

Harold's hands reached around the man's waist and gripped his buttocks. Melissa leaned forward and did the same. The material of the condom had a mildly artificial flavour, but her tongue could not detect any difference in texture. Her attendant's penis was large and thick, and seemed to fill much more than just her mouth. Her nose filled with the musky odour of sexual arousal.

After only a few moments, Harold's attendant withdrew his penis from Harold's mouth and sat back down on his heels. She withdrew her mouth from her attendant's penis and waited.

Harold's attendant produced another foil packet in his hand, opened it to display a condom, and then leaned forward to put the condom on Harold's erection. Melissa waited to see who would do what to whom next.

Harold's attendant reached into another drawer of the banquette and produced what looked like a tube of medicine. Flicking open the top with his finger, he squeezed a quantity of clear jelly onto the tip of Harold's penis.

Melissa felt her attendant's hands on her. He was moving her slip up her thighs. She raised her hips to let him bring it up past her waist. With his hands on her knees, he urged her forward, and she complied.

Harold's attendant had put the tube of jelly away, and now turned his back to Harold. The man's buttocks were small but plump, almost girlish. Harold put his hands on the attendant's hips and drew the man toward himself. Melissa was so hypnotised by the sight of the man's buttocks approaching her fiancé's erect penis that she barely noticed that her own attendant had placed his penis at the mouth of her vagina.

With an ease that surprised Melissa, Harold's penis slipped into his attendant's anus. At the same moment, her attendant entered her. His penis was large and penetrated her deeply.

Harold's hands caressed his attendant's body, moving over the man's chest, one playing with a nipple, and the other reaching down and fondling the man's organ.

Her attendant was moving wonderfully, seeming to rotate inside her as he almost lifted her off the banquette with each thrust, but she was as much aroused by the sight of Harold having sex with another man.

She reached up to her shoulders and tugged the straps of her slip down, baring her chest. Her attendant took his hands from her thighs and put them on her breasts. He caressed them in ways she had never felt before.

The banquette was rocking slightly, and Melissa looked over to see that Harold and his attendant were moving in an increasing rhythm. Harold had his hand in a fist around the man's penis, rapidly moving it up and down the shaft. She reached down to touch herself in the same rhythm as Harold's hand. Her attendant increased the speed and force of his thrusts.

Melissa saw the condom of Harold's attendant fill with fluid, and a moment later came a startled cry as Harold reached orgasm. The sound seemed to run through her fingers into her clitoris, and she came with an almost frightening intensity.

The attendants disengaged themselves from Melissa and Harold slowly and carefully, and, like the women who had attended them earlier, cleaned them and dried them. They dressed quickly and gracefully, and left the two of them alone once more.

Melissa felt as if she had just run a long race. She was covered with perspiration, and she was breathing hard. She said nothing. Her fiancé took her hand in his and gave it a squeeze. "So?" he asked. He sounded pleased, as if he was certain that he had at last impressed her. "What do you think?"

"I think," she replied, "we'll have the wedding party here."

Names are for Lovers

Fiona Curnow

The Mae West quote was probably my downfall. I hadn't meant it to happen like that. He walked into the kitchen at the party when I was just at that dangerous level of drunkenness. Drunk enough to feel reckless but not so drunk that I was incapable of doing anything about it. Added to that, I was mad as hell at my lover for having arranged to go off on holiday without me. A dangerous cocktail.

"You're very tall," I slurred up at the blond stranger who had just walked in.

"Six foot seven inches," he replied seriously.

How could I resist a line like that when it was handed to me on a plate?

"Never mind the six foot, let's talk about the seven inches."

This was delivered in a drawl that the even late Ms W. would have been proud of.

To say that he wasn't my usual type would have been an understatement. I go for the lean, dark intellectual types and I have a particular fetish for brown eyes because I believe they burn more passionately. This man was an Aryan wet dream: blond, blue-eyed, outrageously tall and built like a Chieftain tank. Yes, and don't forget the obvious joke about the big gun mounted on the front.

We sat in the hallway with our legs outstretched, annoying anyone who wanted to get past us to go to the bathroom. He calmly and quite openly rolled a joint on the floorboards beside him. It was that sort of party.

"What do you like doing in bed?" he demanded. Obviously he had decided to cut out the small talk.

"I like it best on top," I told him, quite surprised at my own honesty. "And I did once have a lover who made me dress up in sexy underwear for him to take photos of me. Gradually he talked me into taking it off, piece by piece, until he was actually taking photos of me nude. I felt uncomfortable about it at first but by the end I was just so horny that I literally snatched the camera out of his hands and dragged him on to the bed."

"Why did that make you horny?"

"I suppose I felt my body was being worshipped. I realised the power I had over him. That was a real turn-on."

"Sorry, I don't have a camera."

"That doesn't matter. We're not going to sleep together."

"Oh, yes we are."

I didn't find him attractive. I suppose objectively most women would have described him as handsome but he didn't do it for me. I am a great believer in lust at first sight. When my present lover first walked into the room, the uncensored thought that flashed immediately across my mind was, "I am going to fuck his brains out."

"You know what I like?" he continued. "I like to go down on a woman. God, I'm getting turned on just sitting here and thinking about it."

I began to warm to him just a little at this point. Any man who could actually enjoy what most of them see as a chore, on a par with washing out the grill pan, must have something going for him.

"Would you like an introduction to my friend?" I asked suddenly. "She's not seeing anyone at the moment."

This was not as unselfish as it sounded. Most of the people at that party knew both me and my lover, who was even at that moment waiting at the departure lounge to leave the country. If I went any further, the long knives would be out in full force. "Does she look like you?" he asked, reaching over to touch some of my long hair that was making its way down from its clasp.

"No, nothing like. In fact, that's her, over there on the sofa." Actually, she looked like she needed rescuing. One of the local bores had cornered her. I thought that my new acquaintance would be more than happy to do the job; after all, she might have a plainer face than me but she has breasts that make most men trip over in the street from craning their necks to get a better look. He looked at her for no more than a second.

"Not interested," he stated simply. "You're beautiful."

I knew it was a lie. The standard lie to make a woman open her legs. But it was nice to hear it any way. I hadn't heard it for such a long time and I was feeling vulnerable enough for the slightest compliment to make me fall from grace.

"I want you," he added. "I've got a hard-on from just sitting here looking at you and thinking about what I want to do."

He had, too. I could just see it inside the loose trousers: his body paying mine the most sincere compliment of all. I realised then that I wanted to know more about what was nestling beneath the folds of that dark fabric.

Before I realised what I was doing, we were arguing whether to go back to my place or his. In the end we decided mine.

It was about twenty minutes walk from the party. I don't know if anyone saw us leaving together. At that point, I didn't care. As soon as we were outside, he took hold of my hand; it was actually the first time we had touched and I felt suddenly amused. To hold hands is a lover's thing — warm and sentimental. I hadn't realised this was part of the bargain.

I don't remember whether we talked or drank coffee when we got back to my flat — but I suspect not. The next think I remember is walking into my bedroom.

"Hey!" I exclaimed.

He was lying stark naked on the bed. His long body seemed to take up most of it, more of it than any other man who had ever slept next to me. There was a golden fur over his chest and most of his belly, which I would not have guessed. But my attention was riveted on his cock.

I hadn't been far off with the seven inches quip. In fact, that was probably a little on the low side. I had never seen one that size before — not on a human being, at least. And it was beautiful. Proud and straining towards his navel. Ready for me.

"What's wrong?" he asked, and the proud cock laid its head on one side just a little.

"Nothing's wrong. I just like to unwrap my presents myself. It's half the fun."

The way he undressed me was just right: hurriedly enough to let me know how much he wanted me, but not roughly at all. I wasn't surprised when he began to kiss his way down my belly to rest between my legs.

No man had ever dived into me as thoroughly as this. His

long tongue was eager as it pushed up into me, as urgent as his cock, then out again to flick against the hard, pulsating bud of my clitoris. No man's fingers could ever have been as sensitive, as expert as this. Under the softness of his tongue, my clitoris ached so intensely I thought it was ready to burst.

I imagined for the very first time that I was a man. I imagined I was lying back and a dark, red-lipped beauty was sucking my own huge cock. It wasn't difficult to believe. My clitoris was so hard and desperate that I really understood what an erection must feel like.

Suddenly the aching tingling in that hard bud burst into a wave. It swept right up, deep into my body as if my womb itself was gripped in this explosive orgasm. And right at that point, at that one most intense second, I never wanted to do anything else but fuck this man.

"Suck me off, please," he begged as I began to catch my breath again.

I moved down to kiss his trembling cock. It was already wet with his own excitement and tasted a little salty. As I ran my tongue down the velvet underside he moaned and the proud organ quivered. The head was so huge that I couldn't believe I would be able to take him in my mouth. When I did my jaws ached, but not for long. He was so close to coming that within a minute he exploded, screaming. I felt his penis kick against the roof of my mouth and what seemed like gallons of semen washing over my tongue. He was coming and coming and I thought he was never going to stop.

He reached over to the other side of the bed to retrieve the long joint that he had already rolled.

"Tell me your fantasies," he murmured as we passed it between us. "Tell me the really dirty ones that you've never dared tell anyone before."

"Well, I've always wondered what it would be like to go to bed with two men at once. Both nipples could be sucked at once. That would be my ultimate turn-on."

"Hey, perhaps we could really do that some time. I've always wondered what it would be like to make love to a woman at the same time as another man. Two cocks inside her at once, rubbing together and rubbing her. Oh God, it's getting me going again just talking about it."

I looked down at his cock. I was amazed to see that it really was beginning to rise again.

"Well, if you were one of the guys, the other one would have to be hung like a twiglet or you'd never both fit in. I've never seen one as big as that."

At this, he was fully stiff.

"Roll on top of me," he pleaded.

I was more than happy to. I rubbed my nipples against the mass of golden hair on his chest and rolled his erection against my belly. Soon I felt so horny that I had to do it again and I didn't even ask him what he wanted. I was already so wet that he slid into me like a piston in a precision machine. He felt huge. I felt opened and stretched in a way that I have never been before.

I love to be the one on top. I feel so absolutely in control and I can come whenever I want but I made it slow this time. He cupped my breasts and rolled my nipples harder and harder between his fingers because I begged him to. I rode him like a perfect dance, speeding up, slowing down and keeping him dangling on the edge. When I finally took pity on him and thrust my hips wildly again and again we both came within seconds of each other: astonished at first and then laughing in amazement, like children. When I turned out the bedside lamp, I noticed that the clock said 5 am.

He woke me six hours later with a cup of tea.

"I don't even know whether you take sugar," he said, "so I just guessed that you did."

"You're right, I do. What made you think that?"

"Because you're a very greedy woman."

I was a little unsettled at the fact that he had been into my kitchen and made some tea. I didn't want him to start making himself at home.

"What do you want to do today?" he asked. "Some of my friends are going for a pub lunch; we could join them."

"No."

"You know, this is going to sound awful," he said sheepishly, "but I don't even know your name."

I realised that I didn't know his, either. This had only just occurred to me. I laughed.

"And that's the way it should be. Names are for lovers, not one-night stands. Look, the sex was fantastic, but we never agreed any more than that. I can't have a relationship with you. Don't ask me why."

I didn't watch him from the window as he left the block and walked home. That would have been too sentimental. I hadn't meant things to happen like that, honestly. But I can't really say that I'm sorry.

The Betrayal

Emily Orlando

Angie was singing to herself as she opened the front door. After two months, she could still hardly believe that this beautiful garden flat was 'home'. Robert wouldn't be back for two and a half hours at least as he'd been working out of town, so she would have the whole place to herself.

It had been strange at first. Robert had lived there for two years before they met; Angie had feared that he would be territorial and that she would feel like an intruder, but, as he pointed out, if they waited till he put the flat on the market, found a buyer and found a new place before they were together, they could be in for a long wait. The housing market was very slow, in spite of all the brave faces worn by local estate agents. They had met eighteen months ago, and fallen for each other hook, line and sinker. It seemed the most natural thing in the world to be together.

Robert had been very persuasive. Half the wardrobe, the

spare bedroom doubling as her study, a free hand with the garden, shared household chores, lots of laughter and serious talks into the small hours. Angie felt she had come home in more ways than one. If anyone had suggested two years ago that she could find her soulmate at the local library, she would have laughed, but that was how it had been. Angie was working then in a small junior school, and one of her pupils wanted to do a project on 'Sound'. This had the immediate effect of making Angie feel abysmally ignorant, so one Saturday morning she found herself browsing for books that would be sufficiently challenging and easily understandable for a very bright ten-year-old.

The librarian had directed her to the appropriate shelf. There were not many books to choose from; most were very complex, a few over-simplified. She sighed.

The dark-haired young man reading through a pile of scientific journals looked over his glasses and smiled at her. She smiled back, and gave a little shrug, as if to say "Help!" He saw a pretty, slim young woman, with mid-brown hair with red glints and laughing dark eyes.

He walked over. She noted with approval his tall, rangy physique; his long legs and slim hips. His movements were confident and easy. "Can I be of assistance?" he whispered, his face close to hers. She had been shocked by the physical impact of his presence, feeling nervous and elated in equal measures. She told herself firmly to match his assurance, remembering too many occasions when the presence of a physically attractive man had reduced her knees and brain to jelly. She smiled back at him, looking him full in the eyes.

Angie explained the problem in a whisper. He took the book she was holding, replaced it on the shelf, and said quietly, "Join me for a cup of coffee and I'll make you an offer you can't refuse."

She resolutely ignored all the warnings in her head about primrose paths and wicked wolves. They walked out of the library together. The weather had been dull; now the sun was shining and the street was bright and colourful with shoppers. Robert introduced himself as they walked along, no longer needing to whisper. Angie felt rather regretful; the sense of closeness, the smell of his hair and the lazy laughter in his eyes had been altogether pleasant.

Over coffee, he told her about his work as a recording engineer. He had been reading back numbers of scientific journals to help him with repairs to an old system with which he was not familiar. He suggested visiting the school to talk to the class about his work, then giving extra help to Jo, the child with the special project.

That was how it began. And now they were living together, deeply in love. Angie had never felt so happy. She looked at her reflection approvingly. She had grown her hair, and enjoyed experimenting with different styles. Today it was gathered into a top-knot, with tendrils and ringlets brushing her cheeks and the nape of her neck. She thought of Robert's mouth there, warm and soft, and shivered with pleasure at the thought.

Angie made herself a cup of coffee, and drank it seated on the tiny patio, edged with a profusion of flowers and shrubs in every conceivable type of container. She had discovered that she truly had green fingers, and was now experimenting with growing herbs and vegetables. She was visited by Smokey, the fluffy, friendly cat from next door. He purred and rubbed around her ankles before stretching luxuriously in the early evening sunshine.

She decided to listen to the news headlines. As she moved into the sitting room she noticed that the message light on the answering machine was flashing. As her friends and family got used to her change of address, there were more messages for her, but mostly they were still for Robert.

She played back the tape. The usual mixture: some blanks; someone moaning about how much they hated answering machines and thereby using up all their time; an urgent call-out to Robert for a repair on a recording console; a message from her mum suggesting they meet for coffee; and a message from Tim. Angie pulled a face. She had not been sorry when Tim's visits to Robert had gradually stopped. He made her feel uncomfortable. He was over-familiar and suggestive, but Angie could never quite work out *how*.

"Hi. Tim here. Called round. Sorry to miss you. Returned your tapes. Sorry I've kept them for so long. Left them in the shed. Keep it up, you old bastard!!" The message ended with a sardonic laugh. Angie snapped the machine off, glad to have missed him yet still resenting his intrusion into their lives.

As she retrieved the tapes from the shed she made a mental note to buy a padlock. There wasn't much in there at present, but she'd heard that garden tools were being taken by opportunist thieves, and any way, she had plans to install her enamelling kiln and start working again on her paying hobby; delicate cloisonné work which, recession or no recession, still commanded high prices and praise.

She thought some music would be nice. She looked through the tapes Tim had returned. There were several she really liked: Lou Reed, The Waterboys, Bob Seger and the Silver Bullet Band. There were two of her all-time favourite albums, both by Tom Petty and the Heartbreakers — *Damn the Torpedoes* and *Hard Promises*. She put on *Hard Promises*, singing along, harmonising, pretending she was Stevie Nicks: *'Honey, I've had to live with some hard promises, I've crawled through the briars, I'm an insider.'*

As she listened, she noticed a cassette with a hand-written title... Angie and Robert... and she laughed as she remembered their one and only attempt at recording. She had written a handful of songs, mostly about the doomed relationship that had just ended when she first met Robert, and he, as well as working as a sound engineer, was a mean blues guitarist.

She'd been so used to singing to her own accompaniment of three well-known chords that it had been difficult to work with Robert. She was anxious about her timing, but they'd messed around all day with an old four-track and a drum machine, and she'd experimented with harmonies, echoes and hand-claps. The result had been a bit rough, but promising, and they had intended to try again one day. The thought crossed her mind that she would have preferred that Tim had not heard their efforts, but there was nothing she could do about that.

Impulsively Angie switched off *Hard Promises* and slid the home-recorded cassette into the tape player of Robert's state-of-the-art hi-fi, and lay back to listen, a smile on her face as she remembered how much fun they'd had. The first song was a simple, haunting ballad, and sounded much better than Angie had expected. She sang along, trying more daring harmonies now that there was no one to hear if she wildly missed the note. She was in full flow, when suddenly the music on the tape stopped. She swore. She'd been really enjoying herself. She distinctly remembered that as well as the rest of the first song, there had been three others on the tape. She wondered if the state-of-the-art hi-fi could possibly be doing something as common as chewing the tape up, and crossed the room to sort it out.

Before she reached the hi-fi, however, the tape continued.

She listened in bewilderment. Instead of the singing she expected, she heard Robert's voice, deep and husky, saying "God, you're so beautiful." She was startled; she looked round to see if he had walked in, but she was quite alone. The voice continued, "I could come just looking at you. But we've got all the time in the world. We're not going to hurry a thing." In the background she could hear an old Leonard Cohen song 'I believe that you heard your master sing...'

Angie seemed to be living and breathing in slow motion. Images came and went; she remembered the first time she had slept with Robert, her memories conjured into being by the sounds on the tape. The room had been warm and glowing, lit with candles, softly scented with a joss stick. The sheets on the bed were black satin edged with red. Leonard Cohen's first album was playing quietly. She had been seeing Robert for a few months, trying to keep things light, not wanting another intense, gloom-laden relationship like the one that had just ended. She made herself refuse some of Robert's invitations because she did not want to put all her emotional eggs in one basket. Yet she had been certain from the first time they met that they would be lovers, and, as with everything he did, he gave the impression that there was no hurry; they were free to take their time.

Then, one Sunday afternoon, they walked arm-in-arm round the Tate Gallery, looking for Angie's favourite painting: Rosetti's misty golden *The Wedding of Saint George and Princess Sabra*. She had been disappointed that it was not on show, but thrilled to see so many of the paintings she had studied for 'A' level. The gallery seemed overcrowded, both with people and paintings. She said to Robert that she thought many of the paintings sentimental and heavy-handed, but nevertheless there were some that she truly loved. She was particularly fond of Waterhouse's *The Lady of Shalott* and was touched to the heart when, with a flourish, he presented her with a print of it, and a postcard of the Rossetti as they waited on the Underground. She had been looking for a birthday card for her mother in the gallery shop, and he had bought the pictures as she was browsing.

While they waited they could hear a busker somewhere, singing Paul Simon's 'America': *'Let us be lovers, We'll marry our fortunes together.'*

That had been the moment when Angie decided they would be lovers that night. Nothing was said, but it was clearly understood. She remembered everything as if it were yesterday. She remembered champagne; a slow, languorous undressing; her lying back, naked in the bed as his eyes travelled the length of her body. "God," he had begun, "You're so beautiful."

Then she froze as she heard her own voice, slow and seductive. What had seemed sexy and natural with Robert in the night time seemed banal in broad daylight, by herself. "I'm going to cover your cock with honey, and slowly, slowly lick it off." She listened intently to his sharp intake of breath. She could almost hear the sound of her hair as it brushed softly down Robert's lean, tanned, hard body, '...your master took you travelling, well at least that's what you said...'

Angie snapped the switch off. The silence seemed to be filled with a soft wet sound of licking, Robert's gentle moans and the rhythmic creaking of the bed. Trembling, Angie reached for a cigarette. As she lit it and inhaled deeply, she saw vividly, as if watching a film, the two lovers tangled on Robert's king-size bed; the black satin sheets were a perfect foil for the two silken bodies, hers pale and creamy, his golden... glistening.

Abruptly she thought of Tim, playing the tape, listening to the sucking, the whispering, the soft, wet kisses. She thought she was going to be sick and ran to the bathroom, but she breathed deeply and the nausea passed. She tried not to think of Robert, carefully concealing the microphone, playing the tape when she was at work, listening to it with his friends. Irrationally, she felt really angry that he had recorded over her songs.

It did not take her very long to pack her things and load them into her car. She had not realised how careful she had been not to overwhelm Robert and his home with her possessions. She would not stay and face him; she did not trust herself to maintain the icy rage she was feeling now. She was sure that she would break down and cry, sound as if she were whining, appear gauche and unsophisticated. Either that or she would attack him, nails like claws, punching and scratching, furious and murderous. And if she did, she could picture him holding her at arm's length as she flailed at him ineffectually until she stopped, exhausted. And then she would cry.

Angie nearly jumped out of her skin when the phone rang. She picked it up carefully, as if it might explode. "Hi. It's me. I'm ringing from a pay phone. I'm going to be really late, I'm afraid. This job isn't at all straightforward. It's got to be finished tonight, so don't wait up. Love you lots. Bye." Angie sat, cradling the receiver, wondering if he had noticed that she had not said a word. Not a single word.

The evening had grown chilly, and the light was fading. She drew the curtains, and lit another cigarette. She planned to be long gone when Robert returned. She would drive to the coast, and stay with Lou, her best friend from university. Lou wouldn't ask any questions, knowing her friend well enough to be sure that she would talk when she was ready. Lou had never met Robert, although she had read enough in letters, and heard enough through phone calls to feel that she had. But the two women had not had one of their regular visits since the advent of Robert. Angie was suddenly shocked by how much of her old life had gone by the board once she and Robert had become lovers.

Angie sat on Robert's immaculate sofa, and planned her revenge. She thought about wholesale destruction of his clothes, his records, his furniture, but wanted something colder, sharper, initially invisible. She wanted him to come in, as she had done, believing all was well. She wanted him to realise suddenly that something was terribly wrong, and feel the sick emptiness and shock that she had felt. She knew that he would be shocked; even through her hurt she was sure that whatever he had felt at the beginning, he had grown to care genuinely for her. But whether he cared or whether he didn't, she was full of the desire to hurt him as she had been hurt.

She walked over to the hi-fi, contemplating sealing its switches and doors with super-glue, but decided that her heart wasn't really in acts of vandalism. She wanted to do something that couldn't be put right with an insurance claim. As she stood there, she was overwhelmed with the desire to play the tape once more before destroying it for ever. She pressed the 'Rewind' switch, then 'Play', and listened.

This time she realised just how much of a performance Robert had put on for the hidden microphone. However excited he was, however much he gasped with pleasure, he still managed to ensure he gave a full running commentary for his listeners, And she, inspired by his unusual eloquence, had responded in like kind, whispering lewdly and lasciviously, talking dirty, her tongue as busy as any bee storing honey, probing and urgent.

'...and you met him at some temper where they take your clothes at the door...' The three voices rose and fell, an erotic, pulsing fusion. Angie remembered the heat, the sounds of flesh touching, the salt taste of sweat, the sweet, sweet honey, the hot, moist softness as her vagina closed round Robert's firmness, his tongue, his velvet penis. She remembered he had guided her own hand down. "Let me watch you touch yourself there," he had whispered, and for him, and him alone, she had stroked and circled, her slim fingers sliding in and out of her vulva, caressing her clitoris, moistening first her nipples, then his mouth with the juices shining on her fingertips.

'...then he touches your lips, now so suddenly bare of all the kisses we put on some time before...' His fingers had joined hers, sticky with honey, and then he lapped at her with his tongue, first with slow strokes in and out of her throbbing, contracting cunt, then sucking slowly on the bud of her clitoris. He had reached for her hand, placing it on her right breast. He took the nipple of the other between his fingers and together they gently pulled and rolled the full soft peaks until they stiffened and contracted in unison with the pulsing deep inside her. It had been agreed, without words, that each time one or other was approaching a climax, they would hold back, calm down, then begin again the astonishingly slow and tender build-up of sensation.

She turned the tape off. Her hands were shaking as she lit another cigarette. She drew deeply, her mind in a tumult of confusion. She caught sight of her reflection in the full-length mirror on the door. She could still hear the murmur of low voices in her head, '...and your eyes are wild...' She was flushed, her hair tousled and tumbling, her lips full. Her body tingled, whether with shame or excitement she was not sure. As she stood up, never taking her eyes off the mirror, she saw that her nipples were so prominent and hard their outline could be clearly seen through her silk shirt.

She moved slowly, as if drunk or stunned, swaying towards

the mirror. She looked unfamiliar; alien to herself, sensual. Like a tiger, prowling. She reached out and touched the reflection of her face with one hand, using the other to touch the soft skin around her mouth. Her lips parted, and she moistened her forefinger with her saliva, her soft pink tongue licking her lips slowly and deliberately. Her eyes were dark and unfocused, huge and shining.

As if in a trance, she walked over to the hi-fi, and once again, pressed 'Rewind' then 'Play'. She returned to her position in front of the mirror. Slowly, she raised both hands to her breasts, circling a nipple in the palm of each hand, feeling them swell, imagining Robert nursing, first one then the other, softly pulling and nibbling, sucking steadily until deep in her vagina came an answering throb. She could see his face in her mind's eye, his mouth working for her pleasure, his eyes searching her face to prove that he knew her most secret desires, '...and you wrap up his tired face in your hair.'

Slowly, dreamily, she began to unbutton her shirt, revealing a delicate lacy camisole, clinging to her firm, pointed breasts. She reached one hand in behind the edging of lace, circling and lifting her breast until it was free of the satiny material. The areola was huge and rosy. She could hear Robert on the tape, suckling contentedly, and she licked her fingers before, with her left hand supporting her breast, beginning to pull and squeeze her nipple in unison.

All her senses were heightened as she listened carefully, remembering what happened next. Her breasts were full and swollen; she lay back on the bed, looking at her lover through half-closed eyes. She felt powerful and intensely female. "I love it when you look that way," whispered the tape, "so desirable, so ready. Your tits are so gorgeous — I want to put my dick in between them... I want to come all over them and rub my come into your skin until it shines..."

The shirt and camisole were in a heap on the floor now. Her hands were busy, pushing her breasts together, remembering the sensation of his penis between them, the impossible softness as he had rubbed first one nipple, then the other, with the moist helmet.

Her legs were shaking so much she could hardly stand. She reached behind her and pulled an armchair towards her and sank down, transfixed by what she saw in the mirror, '...and now I hear your master sing; you kneel for him to come...' The man on the tape was saying urgently, "Suck it, oh, God, that's so good," and she could remember kneeling beside the bed, Robert's legs dangling as he lay back on a pile of pillows, watching her take his penis in her mouth, holding her head as she licked all round his balls, fondling the perineum, pressing gently towards his anus. As she sucked and sucked, feeling his penis swell and harden in her mouth, his fingers tightened in her hair.

She was lost in concentration when she became aware of her thighs being parted and a mysterious pressure around her vagina. She realised that Robert was using his big toe to stimulate her, and she wriggled appreciatively against his foot. She began to move her mouth more quickly and suck harder, and he gradually had to abandon all attempts to please her as he became swept up with his own sensations. He lay back against the pillows, gasping and moaning, as his excitement mounted. Just as he felt he could no longer hold back, she stopped moving and looked up at him, holding his penis lightly between her lips.

He breathed deeply as she moved up his body... she had taken him, shuddering and moaning, to the very brink of orgasm, but they obeyed the unwritten rule and drew back. She remembered lying there, exulting in her power to please and arouse this man, enjoying her ability to turn him on and have him begging for more. She licked and sucked at his nipples, then brushed her mouth against his before nibbling his earlobe. She stretched out at his side, one hand resting on his thigh.

"Now you," said the man on the tape, "Let's see how long you can hold out." His hand had trailed down her body, his fingers combing through her pubic hair, his middle finger disappearing into her I cunt. "So wet," he murmured, enjoying his power as the woman on the bed squirmed and moaned, his finger deep inside her most hidden places.

The woman in the mirror unzipped her jeans and discarded them. Her hand slid inside the satin and lace briefs as she fingered the opening to her vagina. The soft lips were hot and swollen, the entrance dripping wet. With her free hand she impatiently peeled off the briefs, watching her finger as it slid in and out of her cunt, the hair tangled and damp, the skin deep pink. Her other hand pinched a nipple. Her ears strained to hear Robert whispering what he was going to do next... she could not take her eyes off the sight of herself in the mirror, legs wide apart, her cunt spread open, her fingers working in and out, then a fingertip finding the clitoris and massaging it. Now she had two fingers inside her... "taste yourself," whispered Robert, and she did. She licked her fingers, then rubbed her nipples, feeling them contract as the wetness cooled. Now both hands were down there, pulling the labia gently, fingers moving inside her, as with the other hand she rubbed her clitoris, feeling it harden and throb.

'...his body is a golden string that your body's hanging from.' Now at last, he entered her. The tape became a jumble... 'your shirt is all undone...', "I'm gonna fuck you till you beg for more", 'and your thighs are ruined, you want too much", "Just do it; oh, do it." Angie could hear his penis moving and thrusting, remember the kisses as their tongues met and wove together, mimicking the movements between their legs. The couple on the tape and the woman in the mirror were moving and gasping and breathing together now, as the feelings grew and grew, building to a climax that would not now be denied. The pace was more furious now, all words gone, just the animal noises of passion, the frenzy of flesh in flesh. Angie could feel her body reaching a peak of excitement... her legs stiffened, she thrust her groin higher and harder and faster until she began to groan and gasp rhythmically as a series of spasms and contractions opened and closed her vaginal walls around her fingers, around Robert's penis, around his fingers until with a shudder, Robert called out, and pumped his semen into her as her vagina sucked at him, drawing him ever deeper into her.

'...and I taught him how he would long for me...' Still naked, still shaking, Angie moved towards the bedroom. Her fingers were still wet with her woman's juices, and as she went she trailed them over the mirror... door handles... books... clothes... curtains. As they dried, she touched herself again, until she had spread her scent all over his room. "Remember me," she whispered, and she wiped her still dripping cunt on his favourite silk tie, drawing it slowly back and forth between her legs. The tape had ended, or so she thought. Suddenly Robert's voice rang out, "Another rousing performance from Hard-On-Up-Yours Prods., this time starring Randy Robert and Amorous Angie! ! ! Come again... and again... and again..."

Angie dressed slowly. She reconsidered her views on vandalism. She found his precious Leonard Cohen recording and put it on the turntable. She held the cassette a long time, until she knew that she would he irretrievably lost if she ever listened to it again. She began to unwind the tape, and pulled it and knotted it and snapped it and stretched it as if she were a spider weaving a web. She turned on the hi-fi and began to play the album, then carefully emptied the contents of a jar of clear, golden honey over the record, the hi-fi, the cassette box. She searched under the bed until she found what she was looking for. If she noticed the thick dust on the tape recorder, she ignored it. In a fury of destruction she smashed, ripped and tore, sobbing at the thought of her soul and body laid bare. She remembered Tim's knowing, suggestive leers, and now she understood.

She found the black satin sheets and cut and tore them to shreds which she placed in a heap on Robert's bed. She would no longer think of the bed as theirs, nor allow herself to recall their long nights of passion.

She re-recorded the message on his answering machine. It now said "This is the number of Robert 'The Rat' Reynolds, an unscrupulous bastard who would fuck your grandmother first and then fuck you. Don't trust him with your lover, your business or your cheque book. Above all, don't trust him with your heart. Thank you for calling." Then she left.

Robert had long forgotten the routine recording of his conquests. That combination of his work and pleasure had been a final adolescent fling, an act of treachery that was only possible as long as he considered women little more than playthings. He had seen Tim's Polaroid pictures of one of his partners. She had undoubtedly believed them to be a secret between her and her lover. Instead of which, Tim had enlarged them on the office photocopier and decorated his bathroom with them once he had moved on to the next woman.

If challenged, Robert would have denied that once he had

thought of Angie as a quick lay. He had gradually learned that he was, in spite of all his bachelor protestations, able to fall deeply and truly in love. When he came home, late that night, imagining his lover lying in bed, eager for his caresses and kisses, he also learned that he could still cry, like a heartbroken child who, with one careless, thoughtless sweep of his hand, has smashed to smithereens a fragile, precious, irreplaceable treasure.

The Ad-Lib Lover

Meyrick Johnston

Right from the off, I figured this one for a teaser. You get so that you can read the signs when you've made it as many times as I have. I wasn't wrong either — although, as it turned out, the headache hit my side of the sack more than hers.

She was sitting alone at a sidewalk cafe when I trickled the XJ-6 past. That's one of the advantages, living in the South of France: they sit outside, and you can drive with the top down. I saw one of those enamelled blondes wearing a see-how-sexy-I-am-but-don't-you-dare-to-touch expression. The accessories included a white linen suit and huge square-rimmed sunglasses. A waiter in a maroon mess jacket was serving her a small black coffee and no brandy. That meant one of two things: either she was on the game... or just on her own.

Three o'clock on a hot, late summer afternoon in a roadside café seemed an unlikely time and place for a business girl. And if she'd a date with Mister Right and he was late, it would have been a Rémy Martin and let him pick up the tab. She looked that kind of girl. But what the hell — I'm never one to pass up a challenge. I decided to give it a whirl.

Two minutes later, I'd parked the convertible and eased myself into a chair at the next table. The waiter was at my elbow. "Coffee," I said, "and a large cognac." The girl took off her sunglasses. I caught her eye. Blue, with a couple of laugh lines white against the tan at the corners. A promising sign. "Your cup looks kind of forlorn, all on its I own," I said. "Why not have a nice large brandy glass, suitably equipped, to keep it company?"

She turned towards me and smiled. She was stacked all right, under that white suit with its nipped-in waist. "You twisted my arm," she accused.

"Two large cognacs," I said to the waiter.

Beyond the palm trees and the promenade, water-skiers carved white hearts and flowers into the blue of the bay. I hitched my chair up to her table and began to talk.

There's a line I reserve for unattached ladies on hot afternoons. Some think it crude, but it pays off. And it's the results that count: proposition a dozen and you might get your face slapped nine times; you could stumble on a couple of eager beavers who didn't rate. But the twelfth time you get yourself laid, and that can't he bad. The way I see it, this is far better odds than I'd ever get in the national lottery.

To cut a short story shorter still, I laid the line on her and talked her into coming home with me. I'm not giving you the patter: it's copyright, and I might want to use it again. Anyway, I packed her into the passenger seat, shoved the lever into first, and left two expensive black strips of Dunlop SP Sport on the hot tarmac as I raced the Jag for the green light.

Most people in Cannes want to live in an apartment block overlooking the sea. I prefer one of those small Edwardian villas behind the old town. It's a cute little place in pink washed stucco with a blue and white tile fresco running around under the eaves. The garden is wall-to-wall granite chips punctuated by mimosas and geraniums in tubs. There's no view of the Med, but it's private. It costs no more than the crummiest two-piece on the front, and there's one extra advantage — no time for a possible conquest to have second thoughts, the way she can in the elevator or along the corridors of an apartment block: three paces from the car and you're in the living room.

Inside, I have a routine all worked out. As I open the door to usher the bird in, I tread on a button concealed beneath the Wilton. At once soft lights bathe the shuttered room in an amber glow, the automatic coffee-maker starts to boil, and the diamond stylus of my vintage hi-fi kit lowers itself into the first groove of Ella's *Love For Sale*. This blonde sussed it out in a glance. "Neat," she said. "Do I get another brandy?"

"On the table by the sofa," I said. "They're already poured out."

"Just my size," she murmured, sinking down and reaching for a balloon. "You must be telepathic." Like the man said once about Annie Ross, she was the coolest thing since cucumbers.

From then on down, you might think, I'd be in like Flynn. But this was the dicey moment: strange birds can fly unexpectedly off the handle — or, like Jacqui, the brunette who knifed that yacht skipper in Antibes last year, they can have your jeans around your ankles before you can say Levi-Strauss. I wasn't one hundred per cent sure about this one, and that's the truth. It all seemed too easy. However, by the time Ella was into *I Concentrate On You*, I'd discovered that the white skirt was a wrap-around. Come the final track and I was in possession of two more vital statistics: she was one of the X per cent who didn't wear a bra — who needs one, with knockers like that! — and the white silk panties had no leg elastic. I was home and dry. Well, home anyway.

The hi-fi clicked, dropping Sinatra's *Songs For Swinging Lovers* on the turntable. Yes, I know you get better repro with CDs, but after what this kit cost — *built-in* Wharfedale stereo speakers, for God's sake! — the compacts will have to wait. And, yes, I know an auto-change wears those old fashioned LP discs, but I reckon that after six well-chosen smoochy numbers the machine will still have an arm free, and with luck I won't.

That's the way it was with this blonde, anyway. She was a natural blonde too, the flesh firm and bronzed around the golden triangle. She must have spent most of the summer at the St Trop nudies to get that full-frontal tan. "Oh, baby," I breathed, lowering my head, "what you do to me...!"

"It's delightful, it's delicious, it's delectable, it's delirious, it's de-lovely!" carolled Frankie somewhere between the Wharfedales. It was too, until a pubic bone struck me a glancing blow on the chin. I raised my head.

The blonde was sitting up. "What was that?" she asked. *That* was the sound of fat tyres crunching on granite chips. I unscissored her long, cool legs and ran to the window. Prising apart two slats of the Venetian blind, I stared out at the familiar maroon Merc and remembered with a sick feeling of dismay that yesterday had been the end of Summer Time... and I'd forgotten to put the clocks forward by one hour.

A car door slammed. "My God!" I gasped. "Wrap that skirt back around you fast — it's my husband!"

Donna in the Summer

Lunar

I'm working my first Saturday night shift. Instead of closing at one am, this place stays open till four. *It sucks.* From behind the desk I'm passing couples keys. Many of the couples throw down three bucks for the X-rated video and are watching *Twisted Sisters* in their rooms. I'm watching the same video from behind the desk and getting horny. As a matter of fact, I'm jealous of every guy in every room enjoying weekend in-room action, while I'm stuck in the office allowing this video to lust-clog my brain and harden my dick.

I could masturbate.

I don't.

Not yet.

Five minutes before four, the Triborough's closed and I'm in my car, exiting the parking lot in cadence with the four-lane highway. Unconsciously driving the green light/red light routine, my mind drifts with *Twisted Sisters* fantasies.

Turning my rusty blue Honda off the highway ramp, I become aware of the nightcrawlers this city shrouds. The result is a heightened awareness and mild paranoia — brought on by the violence these dark roads conjure — before church bells beckon the sun to melt away the shadows.

The reality of this city includes sleepless streets. Such as French Street, my street — known to truckers as Route Twenty-eight — the city's main artery, pumping multi-wheeled vessels through the heart of Johnson Park.

There's the chiffon-laced brute soliciting on the corner two blocks from my apartment. Fifteen years ago *it* was Rutgers' star football player.

She/he waves.

On my block the bars are closed. Inside the all-night steak house, Cluck-Da-Chick, and Muhammad's Pizza, a mixture of staggering drunks, petty thieves, junkies, whores, and homeless congregate.

At the comer of the block, next to the chicken joint, there is a warehouse with four tiny studio apartments on the second floor. That's where I live, behind door number one. Searching for a parking space, I turn the corner. On the unlit sidestreet my car headlights beam a skinny ebony figure crossing the street. As I drive past her working-girl charm, there is an actual welcome to her smile and mystery in her eyes that I've never seen in a street-walker before. Perhaps work's repetitive X-rated video viewing has skewed my perception, but this hooker is new on the block and worthy of another view. Beneath the train trestle I pull a K-turn and head back. Stopping my car across from her, she sashays into the middle of the street and asks, "Wanna date?" Her voice lacks the exaggerated femininity which accompanies the stubble of five-o'clock shadow. *She's real*, young and beautiful with unusually long curly hair.

"Yea, I could use a date," I reply, responding to the biological bulge in my pants, oblivious to the threat of disease and the lack of money in my pocket.

"Twenty dollars," she says in a manner void of bargaining.

"OK. But first I've got to go to the MAC machine and make a withdrawal. I don't have a penny on me."

"You want me to ride with you?"

"Yea, why not...Hop in."

"My name's Donna," she says from the passenger seat. Her red lipstick smile is cornered between the rouged, high cheekbones of an ancestrally proud tribe. "Lenni-Lenape," she informs me.

I proceed to tell Donna that I usually don't do this and that I really shouldn't. "Can't afford to."

We park in front of Rutgers Student Centre – closed of course – except for the MAC machine jutting out of its side. We walk up to the mechanised teller, Donna and I, in the summer dawn. I withdraw twenty bucks and show Donna the receipt with its balance of $3.10.

"That's it," I tell Donna. "Rent's due next week."

"Don't you have a job?"

"Yea… Money flows through my fingers. Can't save a dime."

"Where you work?"

"A motel. Four days a week."

Maybe you need a different job... or two."

I shrug.

We get back into the car and I ask, "Where to?"

She stalls awhile, thinking, then asks, "Ya wanna go back to my room? Sleep with me?" I can't believe it — a john and a whore — "Jeeze, I don't know..."

"I hate sleeping alone... I'm done for the night."

Donna seems trustworthy but most whores have pimps and

that's a person unworthy of meeting.

"No," I regretfully say and follow up with a lie. "I have to get up early for work."

"All right." Donna answers my expected response with resignation and directions. "Drive back where you picked me up. I'll show you where to go from there."

Down quiet suburban sidestreets we retrace the Honda's tracks all the way back to highway twenty-eight. I remain mute as we pass my apartment. At the next corner, Donna tells me to make a right and follow the street till it becomes a dead end. Actually it's a no-outlet apartment complex.

"Turn down the last driveway on your left."

Taking Donna's advice, we descend into a parking lot.

"Over there," Donna points, "behind the dumpster."

Steering clear of the parked cars which cluster the building, we cruise to the far corner. I park my car as Donna suggests. The huge metallic trash receptacle has spewed garbage into the small creek which borders this lot. Beneath the chirping songs of early birds the trickling stream of pollution emits a pungent mustiness of decay.

"Twenty," states Donna, waiting...

From my pocket, I hand her the crisp Jackson.

"Wanna fuck?"

"In the Honda?" I ask in disbelief, having expected a blow-job.

"Yea," Donna says as she slinks her slim body between the seats. "Come on." I can't think of a reason not to as she lies across the back seat, pulling down her jeans with an alluring smile... "Just take one leg out of your pants, like this." Her bony leg looks fragile, varnished brown, with a white sweat sock still on her foot. Her powder-blue panties and blue jeans crumple beneath the knee of her other leg.

I can't resist and manoeuvre my bulky body into the back

seat. I'm cramped, partially kneeling, betwixt the floorboard and Donna. As I unbutton my pants she matter-of-factly reminds me, "Only one leg. It's easier."

"Easier to get your pants on, if the cops come."

Donna giggles, paying me no mind as she unbuttons her white lace blouse. Tits exposed, Donna places her hands behind my neck, drawing my head into her soft breasts. The faint aroma of her cheap perfume heightens my arousal. My lips caress her nipples as my body wiggles a leg free from the Levis I'm wearing.

Succumbing to Donna's fleshly delights, I'm amazed at how simply my body adjusts to the Honda's backseat; from awkward to agile, my body moves across Donna's tempting terrain of womanhood. My waving phallus taps upon her pubic lips before dancing inside the warmth of her feminine pond. Having forged my sexual path, I grind up and down, winding all around as Donna's ass jiggles with rhythmic bounce. Closing my eyes, I feel my face contort against the nape of Donna's neck as her surrounding arms tighten across my back. Breathing compressed, veins bulging — we rock the car so hard, bobbing up and down — I visualise the doors being blown off as my teeth clench and my juices erupt in orgasmic release.

...Listless muscles relax...

Our bodies peel from each other. The sticky smell of backseat sex ripens as the environment takes hold: once again I smell the stink of the dumpster; once again I hear the birds sing.

Now, church bells ring in an early mass.

It's time to go home.

Pants buckled, shoes on, we climb back into the front seat. I start up the car and quietly sit wondering where Donna would like to go.

"I hate sleeping alone," she reminds me.

"I'm sorry, I can't," I tell her and drive out of the parking lot.

"You know, my uncle can give you a job."

"Yea?"

"Yea. He runs the hardware store on Peterson Street."

I drive towards Route Twenty-eight — to the block where I picked up Donna — the same block that my apartment is on. Donna asks me to turn down a one way street, a block from my house. There she has me pull into a vacant dirt lot. Looking around I see the backs of old, decrepit, three-storey buildings with wooden fire escapes.

"Tell my uncle Donna sent you and he'll give you a job."

Donna gets out, her angel eyes drooping with loneliness. "Bye."

"Bye." I wave and drive away thinking about the job offer. I know that hardware store. It's two blocks from my house. I once bought a wrench there. It's run by blacks with a practically all-black clientele. Imagine me, a white guy, in a black-owned store, telling the proprietor Donna sent me. I can just see that fat, old, cigar-smoking uncle glaring at me, teeth clasped tight on his stogy as he asks "How you know my niece?" No thanks, Donna.

As I cruise Route Twenty-eight for a parking space, I remember it's Sunday — meaning I can park almost anywhere without being ticketed. I park in a metered space across the street from my apartment and in front of the Santeria shop, a Puerto Rican Voodoo store. The window merchandise includes candles, incense, lotions, and books concerning spells, numerology, and other means of obtaining health and wealth. Inside its alcove the one-legged Vietnam vet sleeps in his wheelchair. As I wait to cross the street he wakes and curses me.

The guy hates everybody. In the dead of winter I gave him a hat; for Christmas, brandy — and this is what I get in return. I don't turn around, but cross the street and enter the now-open bodega for coffee, a buttered roll and the Sunday papers. Three doors down is my apartment and bed. It's time to rest.

Novices

Carol Anne Davis

On her nineteenth birthday, Bronwen Llewellyn awoke to the fact that it was time to give away her virginity. This followed a night — one night too many — of uncertain dreams, dreams in which a question mark hung over every sexual encounter, every date. Would they...? The slumbering tension, as in real life, had been unbearable. But now, at last, she would resolve it; she would consciously choose that ultimate physical act.

Thoughtfully Bronwen rose and showered, soaping for long luxurious moments over her soft pink areolae and tender vulva. Then she slowly slid into tiny lace white briefs and a matching lacy bra, dressing in the hope of being undressed. Breath coming faster, she stared at the full swell of her well-toned hips in the mirror. Then, shrugging on a shirt dress, she hurried to the shopping centre to meet her best friend, and told her of her plans.

Lynnette, as befit her two years' seniority, looked doubtful. "Don't you think it's a bit... well, clinical?"

Bronwen managed a nervous laugh.

"Of course it's clinical! That's the whole point!" She started to walk along the busy streets. "Don't you see, Lynnette? Most of us spend ages getting over our first sexual relationship. The whole package — first boyfriend, loss of virginity, falling in love — it's overkill. No wonder it so often ends in tears."

Her gaze swept longingly over the couples strolling past them, "What I propose to do is lose my virginity to a stranger. Then, when I meet someone special, I can concentrate on building a relationship without worrying what it'll be like when they pounce."

The wine bar, with the exception of the pop videos gracing every wall, was empty when they reached it. Quickly Bronwen ordered drinks for them both. "Not exactly an aid to conversation!" she shouted across the escalating noise. "I didn't think you came here to talk," Lynnette replied. And wasn't that the truth! Pulse speeding, Bronwen turned back to the barman. "Make mine a double!" she exclaimed in a shaky voice.

She was just finishing it when the first potential recipient of her hymen arrived. Tall and slim, he had the self-assured walk of a Chippendale, strong, even features, softly spiked hair.

"This seat taken?" he asked the girls, indicating the obviously empty armchair across from them.

"Not unless the Invisible Woman's got it!" Bronwen said. It wasn't an auspicious beginning. Still...

"We don't even mind if you smoke," she added, as he lit up a cigarette.

Lynnette stared at her:

"Whatever happened to 'kiss a non-smoker and taste the difference'?"

"That was last week. I've become more liberated since then."

After asking the spiky-haired youth what time it was, Bronwen continued the conversation.

"With that mane of blond hair, I just bet you're a Leo," she murmured, downing her second double brandy and feeling no pain. "That's one of the most sexual signs of the zodiac!" she added with a seductive grin.

"What's the zodiac?" asked the boy.

"No — he wasn't joking," muttered Bronwen, as she and Lynnette made their inebriated way across town. "You just don't get an intelligent class of person in wine bars these days. It's these bloody videos — they've killed the art of conversation stone dead!"

"Perhaps you should join a debating society," Lynnette muttered. She glanced at her friend's mutinous face, "Oh, for God's sake, let's call it a day. No one will want to go to bed with you when you're in this kind of a mood!"

Bronwen sighed. "Tell me again what it's like to have a man inside you."

Her friend shrugged. "Well... you've been through the heavy petting stage?"

"God, yes! Deep breathing, hands under each other's clothing, senses working overtime!" She paused, "And then I start thinking *'will we, should I? Is this all he's really after?'* And I feel so unsure that I end up pushing the guy away."

"I know you do," Lynnette gave her friend a sympathetic smile. "But for the purposes of my description, imagine that you've decided — as you have today — that you're actually going to go through with it. You've got to the point where you've undressed each other completely. That bit can take ages; it's fun!"

She gave a licentious grin, "Well, when you're both really

aroused the most confident party rolls on top of the other and gently coaxes their legs apart: let's assume for the moment that the man's on top of you. He'll probably be very excited by now — well, you both will! — and his shaft'll be trying to find its way..."

Bronwen nodded.

"Penetration! I just can't imagine..."

"It's..." Lynnette frowned, "You feel him probing at your vulva, then actually sliding in. And usually, no matter how wet you are, there's a moment when you're sure that you're being stretched apart, that he's too big. It's best if you encourage him to lie inside you without moving till you get used to this. Gradually he starts to thrust, moving back and forward while never quite coming out of you. It's very nice! "

She realised it was important that Bronwen should not set her expectations too high.

"But most women don't orgasm from intercourse, especially not the first time. So you may want him to bring you off before or after with his fingers or his tongue."

Bronwen smiled.

"Oh, I realise that the Earth might stay in place! I just want to know what penetration and thrusting are actually like."

I just wish I knew what penetration and thrusting were actually like, Nathan thought to himself as he contemplated yet another girlie magazine. The girls were beautiful and, if you were naive enough to believe the blurb, available to every man. But no one told you what to do with them, exactly how to get your performance right, to please. Once again Nathan wished that he hadn't been educated at an all-boys school. If he'd been through co-ed he'd at least know what to say to a girl, if not what to do.

He'd also know where to meet the opposite sex, since bars were clichés, discos a dead end. As for meeting the opposite sex at night classes — so far they'd produced three A-Levels and not much else.

If only he could sit an exam in losing his virginity! Nathan smiled to himself. No, losing it implied carelessness, and he certainly wasn't guilty of that. Rather he wanted to give it away — if anyone would take it off his hands, or rather his cock. En route to the library, he wondered when that blessed hour would come.

"He looks ideal."

Lynnette nudged her friend as a medium-built man carrying a copy of The Kinsey Report walked past them.

"Follow that sexpert!" she whispered, and, giggling, the two girls turned on their heels.

Five minutes later, when their prey disappeared into the library, Lynnette produced a ticket and they followed him in. Then Bronwen lost her nerve. "Changed my mind," she gasped, as the Dutch courage began to dissipate. "I'm going home."

Wildly she turned on her heel, and almost crashed into a thoughtful-looking youth.

"Sorry," Nathan said. He took a step to one side just as Bronwen did likewise.

"Sorry," they grinned again, stepping with identical haste the other way.

"You go this way and I'll go that," Bronwen said, pointing. Successfully they concluded their little dance.

Bronwen left the building and Nathan entered it, each wondering why they always seemed to be going in the wrong direction from fanciable types. A bell, pealing round the building, made the youth jump.

"Fire alarm," the doorman said officiously. "Everybody out!"

Seconds later, Nathan walked past the girls, and stopped for a few words. "A fire alarm," he said. "I'll just have to wait it out in that coffee bar across the road."

"Bronwen," Lynnette said, "was about to go there too. Weren't you, Bron?"

Bronwen blushed.

"They do great meringues," Nathan added.

"Bronwen loves meringues," Lynnette grinned.

Never are we so unlike ourselves as when we're trying to make a good impression. Consequently Nathan had rarely seemed so confident, or Bronwen so sexually sophisticated, in their entire lives.

She must have had lots of lovers, Nathan thought, envisaging a line of rampant cocks before him. *She'll want someone who can really make her body come alive.*

Bronwen sipped at her coffee. *He's obviously been around a bit,* she thought nervously. Draining their cups, they smiled at each other and their new false selves.

"I'll take you home," Nathan volunteered eventually. "It's getting dark."

During the walk to her flat he told her about his love of cooking (true) and cinema (also true). He briefly dwelt upon his busy social life (not always true) and his macho love of hang-gliding (absolute bloody rubbish). Not wishing to seem gauche, he also hinted at two recent affairs.

Fooled into believing that here was a sophisticate, Bronwen spoke of her hectic nightlife existence and recently ended romance, pitting hope against hope that none of her flatmates would tell him that the most energetic thing she did was watch the aerobics championships on TV.

Reaching her flat they found the kitchen mercifully empty, with sounds of life coming from the other rooms.

"My flatmates," said Bronwen. "We're at University together."

"Reading what?"

"English literature and philosophy."

"Oh, I love words," Nathan said.

"*Bugger!*"

Nathan jumped and stared at Bronwen in surprise.

"Sorry, I didn't mean you," she said, staring a the suddenly-dead kettle.

"It's the electricity. The meter's just run out." She dug into her purse.

"Don't have change for a fiver, do you?"

"No, but you're welcome to these."

In trying to hand some coins over, Nathan's hand brushed hers, and a man-made tingle ran through them.

"Oh, I couldn't," Bronwen said, "You've already paid for the coffee and cakes."

Nathan smiled. "It's my birthright," he said. "That's what the name Nathan means — a gift."

Bronwen knelt by the meter and fed in the coins.

"Bronwen," she said, "means white breast." Nathan took a deep breath: "And is it?"

Bronwen closed her eyes and opened her lips. It was now or never: "Why not come into the bedroom and find out?"

Buttons, fasteners, zips being undone. Hands eagerly sliding clothing free of another's flesh. Kissing Bronwen, Nathan's shaft rubbed against her lower belly and his balls moved between her thighs. His scrotum tingled, trembled, tightened. Within moments he spurted across the quilt that graced the bed.

"Now I can concentrate on you for a while," he said, stroking her with genuine admiration, exulting in the feel of woman's flesh beneath his fingers at last.

Whimpering her pleasure, Bronwen kissed him back, mouth parting further. This was to be no rush job, then, but the kind of session in which foreplay went into extended time.

"I like having my stomach stroked," she said shyly, drawing his palm to her warm silk planes.

A long time later, when Bronwen had begun to make upward thrusts with her hips, when even the slightest caress of her stomach brought a corresponding strand of wetness down below, Nathan covered her body with his. With his knee he pushed her legs open, and with one hand he prepared to guide himself in.

"Wait!" Bronwen reached out and opened the bedside cabinet, quickly taking a condom from its slender box. Impatiently she peeled back the wrapping with her teeth. Suddenly she had no idea what came next. "Can you put it on?"

Nathan gulped, nodded, trying to keep his breathing from going into overdrive. He'd practised with condoms at secondary school, and had found it relatively easy to roll one on.

"Done it!" he whispered, sliding the rubber over his exquisitely excited shaft before entering her.

"Success!" Bronwen breathed, lifting her hips to meet his. From then onwards, it was pretty much as Lynnette had predicted — the feeling of being filled, of someone moving inside you, of their pushing forward as they came. Nathan cried out, gripped her back: she felt as if she'd given him a great gift, and given it willingly.

"I'd like you to come too," he gasped a few minutes later as his sated sex shrank and he reluctantly withdrew.

Eagerly Bronwen guided his hand to her clit and showed the sort of movements she needed.

"Not too hard," she said tremulously. "It's delicate, you know!"

His own balls reeling from their recent explosion, Nathan nodded. "Like this?"

Bronwen moaned her assent. His middle fingers moved round and round and round. She opened her legs more widely.

"Just... yes! Yes!"

Like doing it yourself, only you could concentrate fully on the pleasure. Almost... almost... She whimpered as the rhapsody thrilled through her, new heat springing up under his hand.

"Don't stop!" she whispered. She saw images of his hard-muscled bum beneath her hands, his cock throbbing its need of her. Pictured his delicate yet hirsute balls, the sensuous beauty of his full mouth as he came.

"I'll stroke you all night," murmured Nathan, "all the next day — as long as you want it." And, wanting it, she came and came and came.

"God, I'm so glad I went to the library today!" she told him much, much later.

"So am I."

"To think if I'd stayed at the wine bar, I would never have met you, never have..." She broke off, then realised she wanted to tell him the truth, "...never have lost my virginity," she finished softly, holding him tight.

Nathan propped himself up on his elbow and stared at her: "Your *virginity*? But there was no pain, no blood!"

Bronwen smiled.

"There often isn't. I've been riding a bike for years, used to get rides on my cousin's horse..."

"So you lost your hymen that way?" Nathan said slowly. He blinked again, "But why to me — I'm not exactly a stud!" He caught Bronwen's surprised look, and added, "Am I?"

"You were brilliant!" Bronwen said. "I couldn't have given

my maidenhead to a more thoughtful guy!" She sobered slightly. "My main objective was to get it over with — I didn't expect to enjoy myself as well." She smiled at him gently. "I thought that if I gave away my virginity to a stranger it would make life simpler when the time came to fall in love."

Nathan tensed. "So it's wham, bam, thank you, my man?"

Beginning to tense up herself, Bronwen shook her head:

"Not unless you want it that way. Now that we've... I feel close to you. I definitely don't want this to end."

Nathan nibbled the tips of her swollen breasts then began to trail his tongue slowly down her sweat-slicked torso.

"If you're still a virgin to the lick of love you might need me for some time..."

Bronwen sighed her gratitude. She realised she was a novice at outdoor sex, at sex in the shower, sex during her period. She opened her mouth to say so, then groaned and shut it again. For Nathan's mouth on her lower lips was doing more than enough talking for both of them. And her body was finding a whole new language of its own.

Today she'd turned nineteen, lost her virginity and found a most enthusiastic lover. Writhing blissfully against his tongue, she wondered what her twentieth birthday would bring.

The Paris Craftsman

Lucienne Zeger

The Rue de L'entrance was to be found on the southern edge of the great city of Paris. It was an unimportant street of small dilapidated houses long past their best, if they had ever had a best. Cats sat on hot stones to drink in the noon sun and a midday silence more suited to a small village lay over the area. Alison parked her small red sports car as near to the building she sought as possible. She crossed the road to the paint-peeled door marked with a number nine. After hesitating, she knocked hard and waited. There was a long pause, and she had just raised her hand to knock again when she heard a noise from within. The man who opened the door to her was short, bent, old and foreign. "Herr Kraftsman?" she enquired.

He nodded through half glasses.

"Alison Kwik," she said, extending a hand which he did not take. "Come in," he said in a thick German accent.

He led her into a dark and dirty hall. Instantly the cool air was full of the smell of leather, stacked along the walls were large rolled hides in many colours and ahead was a narrow staircase, equally ill lit. The old man went ahead and up the stairs and she followed. At the top he disappeared through a half-opened door. She slowly followed and found herself in a strange and crowded room. It was at the rear of the building and light flooded in through a large, dust-encrusted skylight set partly in the roof. All around were cluttered work benches covered in strips of leather and gleaming tools polished with constant use. The sweet smell of leather hung heavily in the air, full of sensual animal power. Herr Kraftsman had by now seated himself in a position of authority on a tall stool at a far bench.

"So you have come for one of my little toys?" he asked, his eyes sparkling with an excitement not suggested by his age.

Alison agreed with him, feeling both embarrassed and excited by the situation she found herself in. Though there was still a strong hint of the active male in the old man, there was also the professional detachment that all specialists cultivate. With the ease of long experience and complete familiarity with the difficulties almost all his clients found with the situation for the first time, he launched into his familiar routine. First he seated her by pointing to the only other chair in the room, then with delight he started to describe his service in detail. "You could have a half harness but that would not be for some one as beautiful and so well created by nature as you. No, for you" — here he paused to give effect to his consideration — "No, for you, a full and very elaborate harness is the only one. You are fit and young and would be a perfect body for something so wonderful and so demanding."

"Now," he paused again, holding his chin with his hand, "we must consider the most important of considerations. Will you require a female as well as a male extension?" Before Alison could even begin to answer, he answered for her.

"Yes, again you are someone who will most definitely want a female extension and, if you don't mind me being blunt, we will have to consider both size and shape. In fact to do this correctly and to give you my best work, I must be permitted to measure everything."

He held up his hand to suggest protection or reassurance. "My clients trust me, and I am sure that you will be no different. I have been recommended to you and for me to do my best for you, we must trust each other."

At this point Alison felt that she had better say something.

"Herr Kraftsman, I would not be here unless I was willing to undertake what is necessary to possess an example of your extraordinary skill. I will, of course, be only too pleased to co-operate with you to achieve this."

"Good, good, we understand each other. Then we must get on. I regret, my facilities are very limited," he gestured around the room. "May I ask you to remove all your clothing. While you do this, I will get some things together so that I can take my measurements."

Alison found the moment and the request stimulating. This was certainly no doctor's surgery but the same detached pressure to conform was there and felt. She had undressed in front of many men but this was hardly that — more like a dressmaker but even then different.

Herr Kraftsman turned away and started to gather together a number of obviously essential items. Alison set about undressing. Fortunately, she had on only casual clothes. First she looked around to find a place to put them. Seeing nothing obvious, she opted for the already crowded bench. With slightly false confidence, she pulled the tight cashmere sweater over her head. The soft material rubbed gently over her hard nipples. The cool air of the room felt fresh on her bare breasts. They delighted her and those who were allowed to play with them, male or female. Hard, high and very round, they were a little larger than her slim, long frame suggested. Next she unlaced her high-heeled boots, pulled them off and placed them neatly under the bench.

She had to stand to remove her tight jeans. She pulled them with difficulty down her long legs and had to hop to keep her balance. She was left with her small plain thong, the cord at the back disappearing between her round cheeky bottom, the thin material at the front cupping the distended mound and slightly moist where it slipped between the pouting lips.

The progress of the undressing had not escaped the alert eyes of Herr Kraftsman, "Everything, please, young lady; everything." He made a slight movement of his hands and Alison looked down at the brief white covering and the pink pop socks.

"You can leave the socks on," said Herr Kraftsman, as though such a concession would ensure her modesty.

Alison slipped her thumbs through the thin elastic and in one movement pushed the thong down to her feet, where she kicked it free. She stood up, legs slightly parted, to confront Herr Kraftsman with the delicately trimmed and most minimal crowning of pubic hair over the powerfully displayed and lustful mouth of her vagina.

"Few," said Herr Kraftsman, "of my many clients could be considered more worthy an owner of my talents than you." His eyes shone and his face beamed with the obvious appreciation of a connoisseur. Alison always liked a compliment, and smiled shyly back at him.

"Now to work. First we will measure the female requirement." He turned back to his bench and picked up a beautiful veneered box bound with brass corners. This he placed on a table and with care raised the lid. The long box was lined with dark blue velvet and held in individual compartments perhaps a dozen beautifully shaped red leather dildos in ascending order of size. Herr Kraftsman repeated the display with another identical box. This, however, contained similar objects that differed in having exaggerated heads at the end of each of their lengths.

"We have, young lady, two choices in this department. First that of size and then between the one of even diameter and the one with the full head. The only way to choose is to try, otherwise I have found that sometimes a woman's eyes are bigger than, shall we say, her stomach. May I also hasten to assure you that though these samples have experienced many trials, they are always cleansed most thoroughly with surgical spirit. The leather from which they are made, and from which the one I make for you will be made, is of the finest quality, as soft as the place it must enter and yet almost totally water proof. I fill the sheath with my own preparation, which permits some flexibility and feels most natural. You may also consider if you require the device only to fill the vagina or to be more dramatic and pass through the mouth of the cervix and beyond. You may also have one fitted to enter your rear passage as well."

Alison was by now very wet and very open. This almost clinical talk on such an erotic theme was deeply stimulating. Her hole, in fact holes, craved to be filled by the objects that she saw laid out so invitingly before her. It was like a sweet shop and she a child with pennies to spend. What to try first?

"I think I would like a head on the item, and I think that I would like one for my bum as well." She hesitated, hovering over the boxes.

"Take one," encouraged Herr Kraftsman.

Her hand reached out and moved over the box back and forth. Then, with decision, it alighted and removed a substantial dildo. Its leather inviting, warm to the touch and softer even than cashmere. She brought it instinctively to her nose and breathed deeply of its rich smell. Her mind visualised the pink, wet and hairy slits that this had already entered and she trembled at the thought of driving this hard monster in, pushing and twisting it as the recipient thrust back and twisted, skewered upon its attack. She moved it away from her and as it passed her mouth her tongue licked out to caress the large round end.

Now oblivious of Herr Kraftsman and yet aroused by the audience, she brought its head down to meet her own cunt. To make the entry possible she arched her hips forward, bending and opening her legs.

This movement had the effect of opening her hole, and as she drew the soft leather between her lips for the first time, letting the liquids wet it, the need to plunge it in became very strong. Still, as though in a greeting, she let it rub against her clitoris and this touch sent its own messages throughout her body.

Then it was in. At first she felt that she had been too greedy. As her hand and arm forced it in and upward, she felt herself stretched as she had never been stretched before. She could feel it pass the inner gate with just a little pain and then it was onward. As only the last few inches of the massive device were left as a bright red circle framed in the distended mouth, she was aware of Herr Kraftsman close by her.

"May I make some checks young lady?" he said in his professional voice.

"Yes," agreed Alison.

He bent his head as she held her position, standing thrust forward with her legs well parted. She felt his hand touching and testing, then his skilled craftsman's fingers sliding between the dildo and the wall of her vagina, increasing the stretch significantly. Then the fingers were withdrawn and the hand moved with moist fingers up over her mound to the area of her womb. Here it pressed, just above the pubic bone. She was aware of his other hand on the end of the dildo and then its movement of the device, so that it pushed out hard against her skin. Still holding her in this way, he looked up at her face.

"If you were an adventurous girl, you could in my considered opinion get the greatest pleasure from the next size up. You are young and very accommodating. This one you would soon become comfortable with; the next size would always provide a challenge."

Without waiting for an answer, he gently pulled the dildo from her body with little twisting motions that thrilled her. Accepting that the matter had already been decided, he turned and placed the used dildo, now wet and gleaming, on a sheet of plastic and selected the next in line. There was a decided jump in the increments of size and this one looked quite impossible — more a device of punishment than of pleasure.

He handed it to Alison. "Go on, you will learn to enjoy it – even worship it. I know these things; it is my trade to know women's needs."

Alison took it and tried not to look. She knew that this too had been elsewhere and if another had been able to accept it then she would not be beaten and not admit defeat in front of this old man. It was worse and there was pain, but she had never contemplated the incredible feeling of being filled in this way; she could not restrain a gasp. She had not made this journey to this place, to this man, to find anything less than the total experience. This was an essential part of it, this size was to be hers. There were even larger ones in the box. Who they were for she dared not think. Herr Kraftsman again went through his methodical examination. She cried out a little as his fingers distended, probed and searched.

"This is yours my dear, of this there is no doubt. In the future, when you are in your private world, you will thank me."

Alison believed that she would.

She sat back on the chair after removing the monster, to regain something of her composure. The old man searched for another item and produced a tube of proprietary genital lubricant. He now selected a red dildo — this one was quite small — and handed it to Alison.

"For the other hole, it is better that it is not too large, so that it can move freely as your body moves; this will give much more sensation."

He passed her the tube, and she anointed the small shaft with gel and, standing up again, she bent forward so that she could reach round and insert it.

"Don't lose it," cautioned Herr Kraftsman. She smiled at this remark.

"Does it fit well?" he asked.

"Oh yes, very well," answered Alison. The strange and pleasurable sensation of anything pushed into her bottom was always a little joy.

She withdrew it and placed it alongside the other two on the plastic sheet.

"This one is best for your partners," he said, selecting a headed one of medium size. "Unless you have a specific situation in mind, this size is usually universally acceptable in both positions. As it will be the active device, it is best if it is not too large, as men especially become frightened." A smile broke on his face for the first time as he made his no doubt often repeated joke.

He now picked up both a well-worn pad and an even more worn tape measure, together with a felt pen.

"Stand up very straight if you will, and part your legs. Lift your arms out from your sides and please keep very still so that my measurements will be exact."

Standing as she was instructed, the measurement was a further stimulating experience, for she could feel her juices trickling down her inside thigh and could smell her body even over that of the leather. Sweat, sex and leather made a heady perfume, she thought.

He was making little marks with the felt pen and running the tape across her skin. He missed nowhere. Even her hard nipples were marked and measured, the curve of her breast, the distension of her buttocks, down between to find her anus and on again to find her hole, marked for measurement in both cases by the insertion of his finger a little way.

When he was finished, he told her in a matter-of-fact way that she could get dressed. Alison was exhausted. She had been held at a pitch of excitement for quite some time and now felt as though she had been taken.

The selection of the harness style was undertaken from illustrations in a well-thumbed and dog-eared book. The different styles had been modelled by a blonde, attractively figured young woman, but indifferently photographed to create that slightly tacky feel to the images. Alison selected, with considerable and forceful advice, a harness that started with her head, which was to be encased in a box of leather straps. Provision was made for a gag to be incorporated if desired. A tight and high leather collar would encase her neck and then the straps would encircle her breasts, leaving the ends exposed. Dramatic and attractive straps fanned out and down her body, first to restrain the waist and then to lace across the curve of her womb, at the base of her mound. The male dildo would be directly mounted over her clitoris. Also positioned here was a special rubber pad with a cluster of little fingers that would press upon her button as she exerted her own force of the thrust. A wide and parting strap would pass between her legs, holding both her own internal devices. Movable fastenings ensured that these would be given some motion as the male dildo was used.

Alison could not wait to have this wonder in her possession, though it was some months before she received a small engraved card to advise her that it was ready for collection. The difference now was that the address for collection was quite different and the time was in the evening.

She arrived at a very select block of Paris apartments and took the caged lift to the third floor. The brass fitted door was opened by an attractive and smartly dressed woman.

"Alison Kwik?" she enquired with a French accent, and Alison answered that she was.

She was ushered into a small reception room of some quality. Herr Kraftsman stood up to greet her. He now wore a moderately respectable suit.

"Ah, my dear young lady, such a pleasure to meet you again. Part of the substantial sum that my clients pay for my work is to provide them with an initial trial — should, of course, they so wish. Always I find that a little guidance is needed in the fitting of the harness and it is important to me at the level of satisfaction at which I desire to work that they feel that all is satisfactory and comfortable. This cannot be achieved without the practical use of the garment. Therefore, Madame Visage" — he gestured towards the woman who had opened the door

— "helps me in this matter, in return of course for a professional fee for her special services."

Alison looked with now greater interest at the woman. She was perhaps in her middle thirties, with a slim and well-proportioned body. Her high cheek bones, restrained dress and hair in a tight bun all gave her a look of refinement and quality edged with a touch of the severe.

"Are you happy with this arrangement?" the woman asked Alison.

"Oh yes, I am pleased to go along with whatever Herr Kraftsman has arranged."

"Then please follow me," said Madame Visage, and opened the door into the next room. The old man and Alison followed.

The room was a softly lit old Paris boudoir rich – warm and private. Alison saw immediately, lain across a divan, the object of the occasion — the red leather harness.

The woman took charge of the situation.

"Perhaps, Ms Kwik, you would be so good as to undress, so that Herr Kraftsman and I can fit you with his special garment."

As with the first encounter, Alison felt detached and propelled along by the confidence and experience of others to whom this seemed routine. It was exciting, this surrender of choice. Tonight she had worn a dress, stockings and court shoes. While both the old man and the woman watched, almost impatiently, she undressed, placing her clothes with care and trying to retain some dignity. Even when she had removed her little silk top and matching knickers, she was still faced with the removal of her stockings and belt. This time she was completely nude, without even pop socks. The woman appraised her with a moment's detachment and then picked up the harness. It was quite beautiful, complex and even intimidating. The red leather organs that were intended for her looked even bigger than she remembered them to have been.

"We will proceed with the fitting, if you please. Stand legs parted and arms out, and I will do the rest," instructed Madame Visage. Alison complied and Herr Kraftsman sat down a little way away, no doubt to watch with craftsman's pride the demonstration of his work. The harness detached into two halves and Madame Visage started by fitting the top. Alison felt the initial feeling of being encased as the straps were fastened around her head. The neck collar was drawn tight and she felt the way that it forced her head to stay erect. The woman worked quickly and with experience, the many little buckles fastened with ease by her nimble fingers. Alison could feel her torso being encased. Her breasts rose and were divided to point out to the sides. She saw how stiff the nipples had become and all around her was the smell of leather and the subtle perfume of Madame Visage. The woman now tightened the corset-like structure beneath Alison's breasts.

"Take a deep breath in and hold it, please," requested Madame Visage.

Alison complied and she felt the woman swiftly tighten the straps across her back so that now her waist was drastically pulled in.

Madame now reached for a tube of lubricant and methodically coated each of the organs.

"This will not be comfortable at first, so just relax. There will be a little pain but it will pass."

Alison did her best to ready herself for the entry of the large dildo. When it came there was no kindness in the entry used by Madame, but Alison knew that she would have enjoyed doing the same. Even so, a little cry, which must have given some satisfaction to the woman, passed her lips. It was worked in until Alison felt as though she would part with the filling force. The one in her behind was nothing like as bad and it slipped in to give her some pleasure.

Her crutch was forced wide open by both the device and the width of the harness. While the woman fastened and pulled up the lower section to the torso section, Alison was able to look down and see the large red dildo for the first time, erect and in front of her, curving up from the base of her mound like men she had so often seen. She was also aware that, at every tremor of the long organ in front of her, the rubber fingers at its base stirred her clitoris in a definite and stimulating way.

The woman now directed Alison's attention to a full-length ornate mirror against the wall. What she saw reflected was a remarkable and totally erotic sight that fired her in a way she had never experienced before. The muscles of her vagina started to work involuntarily on the distending solid leather within it and her sphincter tightened and gripped its plug. As she looked at herself, she became uncontrollably aroused. With difficulty, she turned sideways and saw pointed breasts and the penis in front of the thrusting buttocks. Her head was encased and warrior like — indeed the totality was wickedly war-like.

Without further ceremony, Madame Visage, in the same flat tone, invited Alison to try the harness. As though she had done it a hundred times before — and perhaps she had — Madame Visage bent herself over the raised end of the divan. She reached backward and in one movement swept up the length of her dress and tucked it beneath her. Above her black seamed stockings, Alison could clearly see that Madame wore no knickers. The stockinged legs parted invitingly and were surmounted by a beautiful full bottom of firm white flesh. The legs ended in expensive, black, long heeled shoes. Alison was taken aback by this display, for it was totally unexpected.

Herr Kraftsman watched from his seat.

"Do not hold back; please go ahead and try your new toy," came the voice of Madame Visage. "Either hole is permissible — whatever is your fancy — or both."

Alison moved forward, feeling the difficulty of walking feeling the rub on her button driving her to greater heights. The dildo in front of her gleamed with the lubricant already rubbed on it.

She moved between the parted legs so that she was over the raised bottom. She could see the little hole clearly and in the darker place at the top of Madame's thighs she could see the hairy and wet rear of the vulva. Frightened but determined, Alison gripped the dildo in one hand and supported her weight with the other. She entered its round head into the soft lips that were presented. Then, remembering how the dildo had been forced into her own place, she thrust into the woman with all her force. She was successful in extracting a groan. With each successive thrust, she gained even more response. She held the woman's hips with her hands and moved her own with all her force. Though she was fucking, she was also being fucked and she could not restrain the mounting orgasm that was fed and driven by so many methods of stimulation in her own body.

When she had come, she withdrew and released the woman. She stood trembling and instantly wondering what it would be like to use on a man. The expression on her face was all the real thanks that Herr Kraftsman needed. This work was so much more rewarding in his old age than the use of his supreme talents on the horses in old Vienna. The smell of this sexual young woman, which floated across the room, blended with his new leather. He was content.

The Smith/Jones File

Tom Edwards

Hardin H. Smith
29 Gramercy Place, Apt 3C, New York 10041

June 1 1992

Dear Ms Jones,

I trust you will pardon my impertinence in presuming to write to you. Since we work in the same office it was not difficult to discover your address which, although presumptuous, is also, I trust, forgivable.

I must assure you at the outset that I am basically a shy person and would never under ordinary circumstances intrude in this way, but my distress at a situation leaves me no alternative.

You must understand that I am passionately committed to personal freedom. So it is doubly difficult for me to raise the delicate issue which is the focus of this letter. But I also believe that problems are best dealt with quickly so as to avoid, insofar as possible, misunderstanding, growing distress and personal pain.

As you will doubtless realise, our desks are opposite each other with only a aisle separating them. Although your desk, before you began work at the corporation, was equipped with a 'modesty panel', as most of our desks here are, yours was removed presumably by the maintenance staff, after the second week of your employment. I cannot understand what reason there could be for this unusual happening, but it has introduced a serious complication in my life.

You are, of course, an exceedingly attractive woman. If I may say so without being offensive, you are exceptionally pretty and endowed with so many attributes which make for femininity, that you have doubtless been told many times that you are quite attractive.

I now come to the difficult part. Would you consider asking maintenance to reinstall the modesty panel on your desk, or at least sit in such a way as to be less disturbing to males? Since the change in your desk's format, I have found it increasingly difficult to concentrate on my work and, further, the situation causes effects physically which makes it difficult for me to leave my desk without a great deal of mental effort in counteracting my condition.

Thank you in advance for your understanding for a fellow colleague in this matter.

Sincerely,

Hardin H. Smith

30 Gramercy Place, Apt 3A, New York City

June 4 1992

Dear Mr Smith,

I am sorry to say that I found your letter both annoying and offensive. I most certainly had no intention of producing any of the results you allude to in your remarkable letter and I did not, I cannot say too emphatically, intend to cause you or anyone else the slightest difficulty, especially the sort you hint at, by having the modesty panel removed.

I did complain to management that the desk's panel was a severe and costly hazard to a woman's stockings, which are an absolute necessary part of a business woman's costume as even you, a bachelor, must certainly realise. The panel has projections which can destroy new pair of hosiery in one slight contact.

As to my posture and habits while seated, those are unconscious and if you should find them offensive I cannot see that there is any reason why you should not avert your gaze. Is gentlemanly conduct entirely absent from today's men and their behaviour? I should have thought your respect for women generally, and a colleague especially, might have suggested to your mind that such a response was the correct one. I am far too busy and too taken up with the details of my daily tasks to be distracted by how I may be sitting and whether that is causing problems for men with too little self control.

I must also say, for my own concerns, that I too have a problem. I did not realise, until I received your letter, that you are not only sitting opposite me at work but that our apartments face each other in Gramercy Place. In the month I have occupied my apartment I have been aware, with increasing annoyance, that one of my neighbours seems something like a practising naturist, which is certainly no concern of mine but it does seem that such a person should have the decency to pull his shades. I was certainly startled to realise last evening that the occupant of that apartment, anonymous until that moment, was yourself.

For someone who never seems to wear any clothing whatever while at home, I find it ludicrous that you should complain that an extra inch of leg should be showing now and again in the workplace.

Sincerely,

Regina P. Jones

Hardin H. Smith
29 Gramercy Place, Apt 3C, New York 10041

June 7 1992

Dear Ms Jones,

I regret my letter caused you pain, I certainly did not intend any such result. Your problem with the desk's hazard to your clothing is unfortunate and your solution understandable. I will, as you suggest, make every effort to be unaffected by your posture in future, although it will be difficult. Your attributes are very distracting, to say the very least. Without in the least wishing to appear impertinent, I am obliged to say that the situation has, if anything, become far more of a hazard since I wrote to you. But I will not, out of respect for you, pursue that topic further.

I was very surprised, to say the least, that our apartments are practically opposite each other but I was not aware that my habits were a matter of concern to any neighbour. I freely admit that I make it a habit to dispense with most clothing while at home, which I find much more comfortable and natural. I assumed, perhaps wrongly, that my activities were too far from my neighbour's windows to be easily visible. I presume yours have one of the few locations where my lack of attire might be a problem.

However, I feel strongly that a person's habit at home are his or her own choice and ought not to be subject to the preferences of others. Further, if I may say so, your advice to me about a proper response to my problem at work is probably appropriate for your response to my situation while I am at home. Also, if I am not wholly mistaken, very little of an explicit nature could be visible from your windows without the aid of some sort of viewing device. Although I did not, until now, realise you were the occupant of the apartment, I was aware that someone was observing my activities with what appeared to be very powerful binoculars. If I am mistaken, I apologise in advance.

Sincerely,

Hardin H. Smith

30 Gramercy Place, Apt 3A, New York City

June 9 1992

Dear Mr Smith,

I most certainly take an emphatic exception to your presumptuous suggestion that my behaviour in the office is making things even more difficult for you. My personal attire is my own business and I will not make any apologies for it. My choice of clothing, any clothing, is my own and I will not alter it to fit the shortcomings of someone who needs to get his own sensitivities under control. This complaint is strange indeed from someone who wears no clothing at all while at home, and sometimes indulges his natural functions while in full view of his neighbours.

Since I am a responsible person, I did not wish to make comments, not to say accusations, about a neighbour's behaviour without careful confirmation. If I used the binoculars it was only for the briefest of periods and I most certainly do not habitually use them.

Regina P. Jones

Hardin H. Smith
29 Gramercy Place, Apt 3C, New York 10041

June 11 1992

Dear Ms Jones,

I think you scarcely realise what affect your presence and posture have on a male. I do not consider myself unusually responsive and I am, I believe, in all respects a normal heterosexual male. Nor can I believe you can know just what your posture reveals to the innocent beholder. My fantasies have been flooded, not to say inundated, by overwhelming data due to your presence. I fear I shall have to describe in my letters just what I am having problems with and why.

If you have observed any of my 'natural functions', as you are pleased to call them, then I am sure you are not doing so with the naked eye (if I may pun about the matter). Again, I see no reason why your suggested remedy is not more appropriate for your 'problem' with my lifestyle, than it is for my problem with yours. After all, I am in the position of having to actively avert my eyes all through the workday, whereas your view of my behaviour is entirely at your option and easily avoidable.

I also find it curious that lately your apartment lights have been extinguished early on some evenings. I might have presumed that you had departed for an evening's engagement, but when I too turn off my lights, then I note that yours come on again quite soon after. Excuse me, but it could be that the binoculars work better and are less visible in darkness. Hmmm.

Sincerely,

Hardin Smith

30 Gramercy Place, Apt 3A, New York City

June 13 1992

Mr Smith,

As I suspected, you are no gentleman. I utterly reject your suggestions that I have been spying on your activities from a darkened apartment. And given your attitude, I most certainly do not intend to alter my behaviour during work time. I would not, of course, welcome any correspondence from you about my personal appearance. Indeed, I think it best that this correspondence cease entirely, as of now.

Angrily!

Regina Jones

30 Gramercy Place, Apt 3A, New York City

July 1 1992

Mr Smith,

I have felt rather ashamed of my last letter to you and wish to offer my apologies for its abruptness and discourtesy. I could not, in good conscience, leave the matter there. Also, since this is a free country, I cannot, nor wish to, forbid your correspondence now. I will not say that I will always answer, and I may not. But I did not wish to leave the matters between us in such a strained condition, or increase personal tension unnecessarily between us in the workplace.

Sincerely,

Regina Jones

Hardin H. Smith
29 Gramercy Place, Apt 3C, New York 10041

July 3 1992

Dear Regina Jones,

May I say that I deeply appreciate your letter of 1 July. If I needed any confirmation of the fact that you are, in every way, the cultivated lady you appear to be, your gracious letter demonstrated and affirmed it. Thank you for it.

Perhaps you have noted that I have taken to closing my draperies these days out of consideration for the sensibilities of my neighbours, and most especially you. Although they are only a fine mesh and allow the light to filter through the windows, they do, I believe lower visibility from adjoining residences, which is the effect I wished to achieve.

At the great risk of offence, I must say that I find my life somewhat more difficult in the workplace lately. Surely even you must realise that your attire has changed in a manner which would be arousing to the most celibate and chaste of monastics. I think even you must concede that to wear underclothing so tiny and/or transparent plus stockings and garter pairs, such as you do make clearly apparent on most days, cannot do less than arouse the normal male. I would never have ventured to mention these costumes until yesterday's fashion style.

At first I thought I was hallucinating. But it became abundantly evident during the day that although you were wearing very nice white patterned stockings and a black miniskirt, with stockings being secured by a black garter belt, and the latter effectively framing the area, it was revealed quite clearly that you were not wearing any other underclothing on your lower body.

I believe it is time for me to state clearly that I cannot any longer regard this as merely an exercise of personal freedom. From now on, Miss Regina, I shall regard any pleasure offered as free for the taking. So be on notice that the traditional constraints of polite behaviour are being jettisoned. So if this is bothersome to you, you well know how to correct my perception of your delicious attributes.

Sincerely,

Hardin Smith

Hardin H. Smith
29 Gramercy Place Apt 3C, New York 10041

July 6 1992

Dear Regina,

Having had no letter from you I presume you have replied in another form: action. Today, the situation, if possible, was worse. Not only were you attired with less than the minimum, but you were even less covered than before. It appears to me that you are now devoid of any of the natural covering on your personal area which mature females normally have and which I observed to be present only the day before.

Delightedly,

Hardin Smith

30 Gramercy Place, Apt 3A, New York City

July 8 1992

Mr Smith,

I do not see that my preferences for attire give you cause to presume anything. Not that it is any of your business, but my change in body hair is a result of my doctor's suggestion since I am sometimes troubled by feminine problems in the area.

Regina Jones

Hardin H. Smith
29 Gramercy Place, Apt 3C, New York 100411

July 10 1992

Dear Ms Jones,

I do offer you my apologies, again. I shall say no more about the matter. It does seem to me that since we work together, and speak with formality and reserve in the office, that these letters are less than an ideal way to communicate. Would you consider joining me for cocktails Thursday afternoon at 5.30 or so? I've invited a few people whom you might enjoy. I promise that we shall all be properly attired, despite my preference for the naturist style.

Respectfully,

Hardin Smith

30 Gramercy Place, Apt 3A, New York City

July 11 1992

Dear Mr Smith,

Thank you for your invitation. I shall be pleased to join you and your friends at the appointed time.

Regina Jones

30 Gramercy Place, Apt 3A, New York City

July 13 1992

Dear Mr Smith,

Just a note to say how very much I enjoyed your party. You have a lovely apartment and interesting friends. Thank you for including me. I enjoyed myself very much.

Sincerely,

Regina Jones

Hardin H. Smith
29 Gramercy Place, Apt 3C, New York 10041

July 15 1992

Dear Regina,

Thank you for your note. I was more than pleased you could come. My friends expressed real interest in you and found you charming. My male friends were also most complimentary about your frock but most of all about your charm and style. I hope you will come again soon.

It has not escaped my attention that your bird watching has resumed. I presume also that since we have come to know each other somewhat better, you do not find my homestyle too repulsive. Indeed, unless my eyes deceive me, you have begun, from time to time, to indulge in somewhat similar styles. You will not be surprised to learn that I find that gratifying. If I may without offence comment further, I note that the remainder of yourself more than confirms the hints I have somewhat involuntarily received in our workplace.

Best regards,

Hardin

30 Gramercy Place, Apt 3A, New York City

July 18 1992

Dear Hardin Smith,

You are such a naughty man. Incurable, I think. I have been somewhat unfair myself, if I must tell the whole truth. I have been, since childhood, an avid naturist myself. I find clothes a nearly intolerable nuisance and was, from my first glimpse of you in your apartment, pleased with the view. There, now; the secret is out. I was jealous of your freedom, I suppose, never supposing one could practise the freedom of doing without textiles in the city. Thus my behaviour at the office. I apologise for the embarrassment I am sure you have endured. You are a good sport.

Very best regards,

Regina

Hardin H. Smith
29 Gramercy Place, Apt 3C, New York 10041

July 19 1992

Dear Miss Jones,

The pleasure of your company is requested for cocktails and dinner at 5.30 pm on the afternoon of 20 July 1992.

Dress optional.

RSVP

Impatiently,

Hardin

Rrrrring.

"Yes, who is it?"

"Miss Jones, sir."

"One moment, please, Miss Jones."

Brrrrrrrrr. Click.

"Good evening, Miss Jones."

"Good evening to you, Mr Smith. Do you intend to greet your other guests in this rude form of attire?"

"There are no other guests, Miss Jones."

"Oh, I guess I was not fully aware of that. I might have reconsidered had I known we were to be alone this evening. Especially since do not know you all that well. I suppose I should not be surprised that you would greet me in naturist style."

"Believe me, Miss Jones, you have nothing whatever to be concerned about. May I take your coat?"

"Thank you. You may."

"Excuse me, Miss Jones, but since we do not, as you say, know each other very well, do you think it prudent to be attired in so minimalist a costume?"

"Minimalist, Mr Smith?"

"Indeed. I think most people would consider a floor-length gown of the very sheerest white lace unsupported by any other visible garments as minimalist."

"You do not, I trust, find it offensive, Mr Smith?"

"Oh, no, indeed. In fact I find it quite exquisite and it raises the aesthetic level of the party beautifully."

"It appears to me, Mr Smith, that my garb also raises the level of other matters as well."

"You are very kind to say so, Miss. I am sure it is a tribute to the undoubtedly miraculous concatenation of ideal genes at your conception."

"You are very kind to say so, Mr Smith."

"May I offer you a drink, Miss Jones?"

"Certainly; a Screwdriver will suit me well."

"Ah, I should have guessed, of course. Please help yourself to the hors d'oeuvres."

"These are not only delicious, Mr Smith, but they come in intriguing shapes."

"Thank you. I make them up ahead of time."

"I must say the puff-topped crackers with a bit of pimento on top are most suggestive. Does all your baking have to do with anatomy?"

"No, but let's say I find the subject challenging. Those ladyslipper finger rolls are a pleasure to make."

"They must be indeed. The shape is one any lady would be proud of for sitting apparatus."

"Thank you. May I ask if you like the carved watermelon as well?"

"Indeed; if running this one over my lips and tongue for the last few minutes is not a clue, then nothing will convince you. The texture is something less than the model, but pleasurable nonetheless."

"Yes, well, delightful. I suppose I should have realised that you were pleased when I noted that your own anatomy was responding rather remarkably, if you will forgive me."

"Oh dear. My areolae always give me away, I'm afraid."

"Beautifully, I might add. And the small pearls of moisture I detect in your cleft seem to be clues as well."

"Mr Smith, you are too observant. I have been wondering for some minutes just how long I can restrain my natural impulses."

"How nice, Miss Jones. I always think natural impulses are just the nicest thing about us humans. I like the way your gown makes quite possible to see the deepening ruby hue spreading from your collar bones downward to the cleft between your breasts. I am convinced that the women who have that special response are wonderfully lively in the matter of natural impulses."

"Unfortunately, Mr Smith, I'm afraid I have reached my limit. Unless I engulf your tumescent member within the next five seconds, I shall scream."

"Gracious, Miss Jones. Let us by all means avoid any unpleasantness, so please do not delay any longer. My only concern is that it may spoil your dinner."

"Have no fear at all, Mr Smith; such an appetiser has been known to sharpen my hunger to amazing proportions. Please lie back and hush."

Seven Moments of Beauty

Sacha Ackland

Smiling.

Pleasure is so simple. One smiles when one feels pleasure, and the first time you smiled at me I melted; just to know I had given you pleasure, no matter how indirectly, no matter how insignificant and instantly forgettable to you. You would not even have noticed the moment, but for me it was the moment all my crazy, childish fantasies turned from day-and-night dreams into real, exciting, possibilities.

It was the first time that we talked, and you will never know how nervous I was, for I had engineered the encounter, impulsively using any available excuse to approach you — I felt like a timid schoolkid, which of course is not too far wide of the mark. God blessed me with the opportunity to jest, and I was not about to let it pass. I made a small joke and was rewarded so magnificently. For a worrying second you eyed me with what amounts to suspicion, as if you didn't get it, but then the edges of your coral-tinted lips curled slowly upwards into a big, genuine, generous smile. I'd never seen you smile before.

For that small moment, over almost before it had begun, my life brightened as if the light of the sun had penetrated into the building in which we stood, and the rays were shining on you.

If only you knew how I longed to kiss you tenderly at that moment, even then.

Eating.

There is something so erotic about food, and eating, that to watch someone eat is a voyeuristic pleasure; it feels like an invasion of their privacy, as if you were watching them make love. Think of a beautiful woman eating a banana. And mouths, oysters, tongues slipping, chocolate, champagne sipping, lips, cream, sucking, biting, swallowing.

It was not an erotic situation. Maybe it's just me; no, it's you. You were in your office and I came in at one o'clock knowing you wouldn't be busy at lunchtime. You were sitting straight at your desk, looking at papers, eating your lunch. I'd never, ever seen someone eat sandwiches sexily before. You masticated and greedily consumed your food as if it were the finest meal you would ever have. I wanted you then. However, our relationship was working only, formal, and limited by the thin boundaries of good taste or whatever they call narrow-mindedness these days. I wished to be that into which you bit so lustily, with your eyes closed, and your throat growling.

I watched, staring and fascinated as you ate, and you couldn't have known what I was thinking, how I was feeling. You licked your lips, so soft, and swallowed with obscene satisfaction. My knees quivered as I was overcome by my own consuming passion and desire, fed by the sight of your tongue caressing your lips as you looked at me.

Laughing.

Not strictly an erotic moment, really — but nearly every one is, the way I've been feeling these days. This was the first time I felt real, true affection for you as a fellow human being – though more than a friend, I hoped. It was something close to empathy that I felt swimming in my veins, on course to my heart.

You giggle like a girl, and I wish you'd do it more.

Holding.

You seem awkward, and I feel the same; I don't know what to do. All my confidence has drained away and now I'm left nervous, out of control. We stand apart a distance, looking away from each other at all the people going by, nobodies, just like us; we look at traffic on the road, not seeing but wondering. We turn to face each other at the same earthbound moment, and I look in your brown eyes, searching for you-know-what. Are you seeking in me what I'm seeking in you?

Now I try to bridge that human gap, and I move in closer, so that I'm standing right in front of you. If you want, you could push me aside and away, or you could reach out an arm just an inch or two to pull me in to you. Our bodies are almost touching. Is it something we're saying in our minds? Instinctively, I move in as you do too, and we touch suddenly but gently. My heart pours forth joy as I see you smile again. It's your smile, you know, that does it to me every time... You are smiling at me, and I smile right back, thinking thoughts which I am too shy and much too young to either voice or put down on paper. It's like you can hear me, read my mind; you get the message and slide your arms around me to hold me. I only feel tenderness for you at this moment. Do you wish to hold me, capture me to keep and protect me? I wanted to be the strong one, but sometimes I fail, and you always take away the hurt in that.

My arms are locked around your waist so tight I am not sure I could let go. I don't want to. I rest my head on your slender shoulder, unable to speak, not knowing the best thing to say anyway.

My smile has faded as yours has, realising that this is serious. I am alight at your very touch.

Kissing.

I turn my head to look up at you, to look in deep, deep eyes. They are small and dark, but they glow.

You lean over a little to put your lips on mine, slightly parted. The so-light pressure is unbearable. You are so gentle, slow and warm, like a perfect dream. You don't let go of me, so I relax and let my body ease into yours. Your lips are soft, like young rose-petals. Smooth. Your mouth is so hot, like a furnace, a melting-place. I want to drown in your warmth. You taste of something sweet, as if you'd eaten honey. I'm smiling inside.

Sharing.

It is our first moment of sorrow together, a landmark of sorts, but not a pleasant one. I feel sympathy, perhaps even empathy, in your loss of a distant, but loved, relative. Death is painful, but it is life-affirming too. I take you in my arms, and almost simultaneously into my heart. It is at this moment that I realise I love you, and I tell you, just wanting you to know, without caring if I hear it back. I know that if I don't say it now I might never be able to. I embrace my own vulnerability, for you. You say you love me too and I know you mean it. But your pain is still there and I cannot make it go away, cannot even try.

Only time heals wounds such as this. All I can do is lend a heart, an ear, a shoulder, and feel for you. If I could I would lift the burden from you and carry it myself, but much as I care, I can't. I feel grief born of sympathy, but I can't heal you. You try to forget, but we both know you can't. You feel that you should not cry because you're a grown man, but you're wrong. And people never stop growing inside.

I want to be your lover, but of course that means being everything to you. A partner to a man is mother, sister, daughter, friend, fantasy; all these first, only lastly a lover. So for your sake, because I love you so, I lose my own identity and become your post to lean on, a solid, unjudging shoulder to cry on, saying "give over to me your troubles so that they may be halved". I take your head and bend it to my breast, holding your hand in mine. You lean heavily upon me, but I am easily able to bear the weight of your body and the weight of your sadness. Love gives the greatest strength of all.

I feel your tears on my skin, and each drop hurts as if it were acid, threatening to burn through to my heart.

At last love. It is dark. You stand behind me so I can just feel your breath on my neck. I can smell your delicate individual perfume; it lingers in my senses. There is a chill in my bones, the cause being fear. There is no need for it, of course, but this matters so much to me. You are barely touching me, yet all I know is that you are so near, your body close to mine. I cannot see you with my eyes, but I can sense, hear, feel and even smell you.

You reach both arms around me and touch my eyelids softly and gently, then my nose, and at last my lips. I feel as if I'm preparing to dance. You wet my lips with your finger and slip it between them into my mouth. I suck your finger as if I were a baby. You lick my ear and I smile. You pull my hair from around my neck so you can lick there too, and you bite into it gently at first and then harder, with passion, and I can't contain a moan. I am dizzy with desire and need, hunger and warmth.

I can feel your familiar heat. I shake. I feel a primal greed. I reach behind me to grab your hips and pull you right up against me. All I can feel is the urge to get closer. You lift up the hem of my dress with light, shaking, fingers, up, up past my thighs, brushing past, like saying hello, then past my hips, up past my waist and over my head. I am wearing only pants underneath, and I can't stop smiling. You are moving so slowly, probably to tease me, because in everything else I always rush you. As I am facing away from you I am helpless, but I stay where I am, a captive. You bring your fingers to my breasts and caress them so softly and slowly, twirling the tips of your fingers round my nipples, deliberately grazing me with your nails. Putting one hand on my stomach you pass over the sensitive ticklishness of my belly so I have to draw breath fast. I lean my head heavily back on your shoulder as I can hardly bear the weight of it. I am almost shaking, thinking, "this is too real". I feel as if I had been possessed but that now I'm really me. I feel insane.

In my ear you whisper: "I want to fuck you"...naughty boy... You move in front of me, kneel down, and look up at me with that look in your eyes....mischief and affection. You look like a little boy whose just discovered that there is more to little girls than sugar and spice. I feel like Venus being adored, but even more.

You move in closer and put your mouth to my thighs, kiss them with ardour. I can't help opening my legs a little, automatically. You push me down onto the bed so that my legs hang over the end. The sheets are cold and make me shiver. It is dark, and I wish it were lighter so that I could see you better, see your face.

Your shirt is lying crumpled on the floor with my dress. In a moment quite unlike any other, a moment which seems to capture all my desires, symbolise my hopes for this, I reach out to you, undo your belt and slide it out. I don't want to think, but can't help it: I want this to be right for both of us. I want to please — please you more than I want to please myself, and so I'm nervous. I put my head forward to your hairless chest, kiss and stroke you, all aquiver. Closing my eyes I give in to the dark, my other senses enhanced. Now you are saying my name softly. I can feel your skin, as soft as a child's, against mine. I smell your masculine scent, more potent than any drug; I can taste the salt of your sweat on my lips and tongue. When I pull at your hair with my teeth I smell it too.

We pull down your trousers and I pull you down on me. There are no boundaries between people except those that exist in our heads, and I let go of those, if only for a while, so that I can be wholly with you. I want to be at one with you — with your mind and soul and body — all beautiful to me, precious to me, and being generously given to me. I am ecstatic already. Don't ever stop. I tremble with passion and you stop kissing me to look in my eyes. What do you see there? I feel your arms around me, securing and possessing. At last, this is it, it's going to happen. My breath is stolen by my own excitement, the rush spreading through my body, centred between my thighs. You slide your head down to that tender junction, and slip your tongue in to tease my clit. I turn and twist but can't escape the consuming pleasure you give with your sweet mouth. I moan and moan, delirious. You drive your tongue in my navel. I sigh, and you flinch because I forget how hard I dig with my nails. I want to engulf you with the flames of my desire, and I cry your name out loud; loud, into your ear.

I roll you off me and onto your back so that I can taste your body too. Starting with your neck and lips I work my way down, touching your hips, biting your nipples, leaving small red lovebites on your neck and chest. With one hand in your mouth I bite into the soft flesh of your lower belly, at the same time taking your balls in my other hand and caressing as gently as I can in my state of arousal. You groan, just fuel to my fire. I take you in my mouth, licking the tip of your penis to taste the moisture there. You are pulling my hair, trying not to thrust, enjoying my ministrations noisily.

Finally you pull me up and roll me over onto my back. Unable to bear it, I wrap my legs around your waist and "Please, baby...." come from my own lips. You pull back a bit to push gently inside me, so, so slowly. We speak in low moans, the hushed tones of lovers, all those corny things we say. I feel so free; making love with you is like flying, but oh, so much better. I dig my nails into your back hard. I have to gasp as you drive into me faster and faster, like ripping open my heart. I hold you as tight as my strength will allow. You are almost screaming. When I come it is like free-falling, like stars colliding; it is like the earth rising up to meet the sky, that explosion of being. I cry out your name and it spurs you on to your own climax, heaving and gasping.

But it's not the end. As you gather me up into your arms again and wrap the sheets around us, both giggling for some unknown reason, I think, it's just the start; everything is just beginning.

The Orgasmacists

John Harburt

A fine spring Saturday morning in London's Regent's Park is magical. The air is crisp and clean, the flower beds are a riot of colour and the trees are dressed in their new spring green. Even the people seem slightly less obnoxious and there are less of them, just the odd jogger, some nannies pushing prams, the occasional pair of young lovers strolling hand in hand and a few local folk taking the air and walking their dogs.

It is a scene reminiscent of a fifties movie, and the action about to take place could have come from the same corny old love story.

Carol, medium height, mid thirties, fair hair, green eyes, more handsome than beautiful, but with a good figure, long legs, trim waist and firm breasts, was walking her dog Charlie, a hairy mutt with no breeding but a great character. Alex, just over six foot, early forties, dark longish hair with a touch of grey, brown eyes and lean body, was walking his pretty toy poodle BB, good breeding but a mean little temper.

It all begins, of course, with BB barking at Charlie and Charlie taking off after BB. Quite predictably, they chase into a small area of shrubs followed (surprise, surprise) by Carol and Alex, who emerge a moment later with Charlie back on his lead and Alex carrying BB under his arm. He needn't have worried, Carol assures him; Charlie has had his pockets picked so he wasn't interested in BB's obvious charms. For him, it was all chase and no conquest.

Pockets picked — that was an expression Alex hadn't heard before and they both had a good laugh at it, followed by a moment's silence when they each looked into the other's eyes, realised that this was something they never normally did, enjoyed what they saw and felt that first tiny tingle inside.

The conversation that followed was all stilted small talk with Alex inviting Carol to join him for a cup of tea in the park café. Half an hour later, after more small talk, they were at the park gates, having learned little about each other except that Alex lived in a small mews just off Baker Street, a few minutes' walk away, where he worked as a freelance consultant. And that Carol lived in the opposite direction, near King's Cross, where she too worked from home as a self-employed consultant.

So they parted and that would have been that, except during the following week, and at the oddest of times, thoughts of Carol invaded Alex's mind and similar curious thoughts of Alex crept into Carol's head. Hardly surprising then that the following Saturday, same time same place, Charlie and BB were taken for another walk and their owners just happened to meet again. This time tea in the café took nearer an hour and the conversation flowed more easily, giving each time to admire the other's good looks and figure, reaffirming their first impressions. As dogs tangled their leads on the walk back to the park gates, there was even a slight brush of physical contact and little sparks of sensual pleasure shot between them.

Alex couldn't let the moment pass. "How about dinner one evening?" he suggested.

"Fine."

"Thursday evening?"

"Great."

"How about San Carlos in Crawford Street?"

"Good choice."

"Shall I pick you up or meet you there?"

"Oh, I think we should meet there."

"About eight?"

"Fine."

"OK, till Thursday."

"Till Thursday."

"Bye."

"Bye."

Like kids anticipating Christmas, the time over the following days dragged painfully slowly for Carol and Alex.

At 10.30 on Monday morning, Carol's phone rang. It was Rashid, a regular client, one of many young Asians whom Carol looked after. Their religious beliefs forbade them any serious contact with members of the opposite sex, so Carol helped them cope with the rising tide of their manhood. She finished showering and changed into the black, lacy French basque, crotchless knickers and silk wrap most favoured, and at midday the doorbell rang.

An hour earlier Alex had a call at his flat. It was Valerie Thornton, wife of a successful workaholic young businessman, again one of a number among Alex's clients, most younger than him but who didn't want to take a lover and had husbands who put work before pleasure. Alex had the looks, skill and necessary discretion to fulfil their needs. Alex changed into the red tanga, jogging trousers, white T-shirt and cashmere sweater that Valerie favoured, and at just after one o'clock, under pretext of shopping at Selfridges, she rang Alex's doorbell.

In expert hands, both Rashid and Valerie enjoyed an hour of sexual pleasure that each could never find elsewhere, as did a whole procession of clients during the following days at the two apartments. Each achieved complete satisfaction and paid accordingly. Yet neither Carol nor Alex reached orgasm, though they sometimes faked it; that was part of the job. In fact it had been years since either had 'felt the earth move'. It seems that too was part of the job, a fact confirmed by their various friends in the business.

Like Carol, most of her associates advertised by using a small one-man-band company who printed labels and stuck them in phone boxes around the West End. But unlike her friends, Carol rejected the more usual and obvious sexual references and come-ons, simply stating 'Professional, attractive, young Orgasmacist 401 5906.' Alex had never had need of phone boxes so had never seen Carol's notice, and wouldn't have recognised her from it if he had. But it might have aroused his curiosity, because his small monthly advert in three local newspapers and magazines read, 'Skilled Male Orgasmacist. New lady clients welcome. Satisfaction guaranteed. Discretion assured. Tel. 553 0802.'

Thursday evening and Alex arrived suitably early at San Carlos, Carol arrived correctly late. Peter, the head waiter, had been primed to expect and welcome her and show her to Alex's usual table. He stood as she approached, took her hands and leaned forward to kiss her gently on the cheek. All quite formally, of course. Peter served them chilled champagne, followed by a superb meal accompanied by a fine bottle of *premier cru* Château Beychevelle '75; no dessert or cheese, but bitter chocolate mints, black coffee and a glass of Armagnac each. As the candles flickered and the wine flowed so the conversation mellowed, the laughter rang and the little sensual sparks grew ever more intense between them. Yet still they discovered little more about each other, except that they both had few friends, hardly any living relatives and enjoyed a high income, which they spent mainly on clothes and not much else, preferring to save for an early retirement instead. And, as already ascertained, each was a professional consultant. Carol also found herself strangely turned on by Alex, a sensation she hadn't felt in a long, long while, and a little moisture dampened her crotch to prove it.

By 1 a.m. it was time to leave and Peter showed them to the door. Outside a spring shower soaked the pavements and the few late-night revellers.

Carol and Alex darted from shop doorway to shop doorway, his arm around her shoulders. Then they kissed. Not hard and aggressive, but slow and gentle. And as their lips still lightly touched they opened their eyes and the sparks turned to flame, and deep inside each a sleeping urge awoke. The time was right. But the situation was wrong. Alex couldn't take Carol back to his flat; she would discover his occupation. And Carol couldn't invite Alex back to her place for fear of the same.

So they pulled apart, holding hands, and made a lovers' tryst. They would meet next Tuesday evening, 6 p.m. at the small but luxurious Sandford Hotel in Peyton Street.

A taxi stopped, Carol stepped in, a last peck goodnight and each returned home with a broad smile on their face and a slight swimming sensation in the head.

Alex was standing at the window of the sumptuous but small hotel bedroom when Carol stepped from the taxi. Even from two floors up he could see that under a light coat she was wearing a button-through red dress. Alex loved buttons; so much more friendly than zips.

He surveyed the room for the umpteenth time, turned the champagne bottle in the ice bucket and checked his tie in the mirror.

The knock on the door was barely audible. Carol stood there and a slight waft of expensive perfume swam into the room. The sense of smell is an important part of lovemaking. For a moment neither spoke, simply preferring to stare. Alex opened the door wider and she stepped in.

"I wondered if you'd come," he said. Both smiled, secretly reading more into what he had said than was intended. "And I wondered if you'd be here," Carol replied.

"Champagne?"

"Please; I think I need it."

"Me too."

He took her coat and poured a little into each glass, waited until the mousse had settled, and then filled them.

"Cheers."

"Cheers."

Carol sat in one of the easy chairs by the window and crossed her slim legs. Alex sat on the edge of the bed.

"Do you..." They both started to say the same thing at the same time and both laughed, stood up, stepped towards one another, placed their glasses on the table and kissed a long, slow, moist and gentle kiss. And for them both, the world went away and they were lost in time and in each other.

Their lips parted. Carol clasped her hands behind Alex's

waist. He leaned back slightly and brought both hands up between them and undid the top button of her dress.

Carol released her hands, placed one finger on his lips and her other hand across the open button.

"Sit," she whispered, "on the bed."

"I'm not Charlie."

"I didn't think you'd had your pockets picked."

They both giggled and Alex slid back to rest on the bedhead. Laughter too is an important part of lovemaking. For a few seconds each stared at the other, smiling. Then slowly, sensually, one by one, Carol undid the buttons of her dress in practised, feminine movements, never allowing it to gape open too far; just the occasional glimpse of red silk bra, briefs and suspender belt. She knew too well just how much the sense of sight added to lovemaking. Turning her back to Alex, she eased the dress from each shoulder and let it fall to the floor. It was clear that she kept herself in good shape, slim and firm. Now she turned and, playfully biting her bottom lip, gently rubbed her breasts and her crotch. As she slipped her hands behind her back to release her bra, Alex could feel his erection growing and bulging in his trousers. Carol noticed too and ran her tongue around her lips, as she peeled off her bra with one hand, holding the other across her full, naked breasts for a moment.

Then, raising one foot on to the low table edge, she lowered her hands to undo the front suspender of her stocking. This pulled her arms together, squeezing her breasts into a deep cleavage. One by one she undid each suspender, released the back clasp and tossed the suspender belt on to the chair. Then the dark fine stockings: placing each foot in turn on the edge of the bed she slowly peeled them off until she stood in just her skimpy red silk briefs, posing and swaying slightly before Alex.

"No underwear," he breathed.

"No underwear," Carol agreed, and, turning her back to him with a thumb in each side of her briefs, she slid them off and slowly turned again to face him.

Her figure was perfect, her skin fine and smooth, her breasts full and firm and her crotch shaved clean like a pre-pubescent girl. Looking straight at him, she slid her hand down her stomach and her forefinger into her moist slit, gently stroking her clitoris. With a soft "Mmmm," she whispered, "OK — show's over; now it's your turn."

Alex stood, placed one hand in the small of her back and the other on her breast, kissed her and turned her at the same time till she sat, then stretched out, naked on the bed.

As a stripper Alex was as practised and skilful as Carol, moving to a slow rhythm with sensuous motion, first kicking off his shoes and tugging off his socks and tie, then undoing each shirt button and cuff before pulling it from the waistband of his trousers slipping it off his shoulders and dropping it to the floor. A few fine hairs covered his solid but not too muscly chest. Undoing his belt and sliding down his zip he turned sideways to Carol, released the top clip of his trousers and let them drop to the floor then stepped out of them.

He was wearing a black cotton tanga which, in his now erect form, was stretched to its limit, gaping slightly at each side of his crotch. Carol couldn't hide a smile. Alex slid his hand down inside to squeeze his penis gently then, with the other hand and in one deft movement, peeled down the tanga and stood naked, placed his hands on his hips, turned sideways from the waist and allowed Carol a profile of his strong, firm member.

A moment later he was lying beside her on the bed and they kissed, long, moist, deep and passionately, his hands exploring her body and her hands his — both lightly, barely contacting the surface of the skin; touch is the most important part of lovemaking. Their lips parted and, pushing him into the pillows, Carol rolled on top and slid snake-like down his body till her mouth was just above his penis. For a moment she stroked it up to the pulsing tip and the most sensitive area of fine skin below before her open mouth descended and her tongue took over where her fingers left off. For the first time in a very long while, Alex sensed his control slipping away. "Enough," he breathed, and, taking her under the arms, lifted Carol up so that their mouths met again and his penis slipped between her legs. Now the kissing increased in fervour and tongues licked in deep passion.

They turned and Alex rolled on top and down on Carol, her legs opening to allow his mouth to reach its goal and his tongue to do its work on her clitoris. And now it was Carol's turn to sense her control fading and her senses tingling until she too breathed, "Enough."

The moment was here. He pulled himself up, resting on his elbows by her shoulders, her hands gripping his back. And as they kissed he slipped slowly and gently inside her and they both let out a little gasp. Deeper and deeper he went until he could feel her muscles inside tighten around him and she could feel him filling her up. For a few seconds both were still, then, as her legs came up and her calves wrapped over his thighs, the rhythm began, not thrusting but gently gyrating, two pelvises in perfect harmony.

Now the tension increased. Now the world slipped away. Now they both started on an unstoppable path. Now the rhythm grew stronger. Now they rose higher and higher. Now the gyrating turned to thrusting. Now the sensation became almost unbearable. Now. Now. Now. Light. Sound. Pumping. Throbbing. Ecstasy. Pleasure bordering pain. On and on. And now fading. Fading. Peace. Silence. A gentle kiss. And another. Still together. Still together. Side by side now. Squeezing hands. Breathing deeply.

Then together, "I think" — a pause and together again — "I know" — pause — "what you do" — pause — "for a living." The laughter that followed and the laughter that would not stop echoed down the hall outside, and miserable old Jack the cleaner growled, "Stupid fuckers."

Sally's Guardsman

S.L. Stockford

Sally blamed herself. If her libido had not been so high (she never questioned that it might be Tony's that was too low), perhaps none of this would have happened. Their marriage would have plodded forward at twice a week (if she was lucky), until they ended up as two wrinklies in deckchairs on the promenade.

She was, she felt, unlucky to be caught. Tony had picked her up from the Christmas party three hours too early; Dave was the dishy, quiet accounts manager and she had got a little too squiffy. She had politely resisted his initial advances, but by the time they had reached the accounts office her head had swirled away on a cloud of alcohol and passion.

Tony came, he saw and he fled, coward that he is, thought Sally. Then he sulked. For three days Sally was tortured by a silent brooding that suffocated the entire house. She was fearful that the smell of burning martyr might even set off the smoke detector. It didn't. Nothing happened, nothing at all. Now they didn't even have sex once a week.

Sally was desperate. Sally was contrite: "How can I make it up to you?"

Tony: "By never throwing yourself at another man!"

Sally: "I promise."

Such promises are often made in the heat of the moment. Promises are mere words used to secure a specific outcome. They could, at the time of making them, be heartfelt, honest pledges totally believed by those reciting them. They rarely lasted beyond the moment.

Tony: "Prove it."

Prove it? How? Tony's bottom lip jutted; another sulk was developing. All right, she agreed. But how, she wondered?

Two days later she discovered how he could guarantee her monogamy. She thought he was joking at first, teasing her in revenge for her attempted infidelity. Once she found herself on the hard leather couch, her ankles suspended apart by leather stirrups, she knew he was serious.

As her eyes took in the pictures on the wall, all of tattooed men and women, she had a slight hope that it was still a joke, a cruel punishment. Indeed she did feel suitably chastised for her behaviour and vowed never to be caught again *in flagrante delicto*. However, after the local anaesthetic the short young man with his ears littered with adornments of every description told her that it was not a joke. The local tattooist was also into piercing.

The tiny steel rings, one in each lip, jingled together, producing an electric tingle as she walked along the aisles of the do-it-yourself superstore. Though it was nearly empty, being minutes before closing time, she still blushed from head to foot as Tony tested padlock after padlock. Some too heavy, others too flimsy; one Sally rejected because it was so damned ugly!

The padlock chosen was a silver steel 'miniature Guardsman'. "Thieves cannot drill through this!" boasted the card in the packaging.

"Ideal!" whispered Tony.

Sally could never get used to the odd, intimate addition to her body. Its weight weighed down her favourite tiny panties, stretching the elastic, and forcing her to wear more substantial large, tight granny knickers. When she walked, sat or even moved, it pulled on her lips.

Yet it was erotic.

It was like having some firm unyielding soldier guarding her most private self. She felt protected and controlled in the most sensual manner. A manner over which she had no say. Tony had the key and he kept it hidden.

However, she had to pay a terrible price. Before the addition to her person she wanted sex once a day, maybe twice a day on weekends. Tony could barely handle more than twice a week. Now she was continually turned on, whether she was in the office, in the canteen, in the bar, at home, or even with her mum. She was constantly reminded of her sex, and constantly reminded of her frustration.

Life became unbearable, a continuous hot frustration. She thought of little other than sex. Tony teased her. She had to admit to being the worst slut the world had ever seen before he would reveal the key, unlock her and then, all too quickly, fuck her: she was locked up so swiftly again she felt that she was never out of bondage.

At work David continued his advances, but with her guard securely in place she could never let herself succumb to his gentle, teasing come-ons. But, oh, how she would love to.

Two months after her imprisonment began, she and David ended up in a bar on a long lunch break; neither wanted to break the sexy mood they had created. They had so much to say to each other, so much in common. She was totally at ease with him, and when the barman finally eased them out of the door she knew they would not return to the office. They spent the rest of the afternoon in his company Granada, the windows steamed up with their passion.

Then his wandering hands found it.

She would never forget his expression: shock. Eyebrows high, mouth gaping. David was always so much in control at work, so calm, so authoritative, but now he just stared. Sally explained the reasons. She was candid about her own shameful passions and her husband's more 'normal' responses. David explained that he found her passions normal. "Twice a week!" He laughed, "I'll be disappointed if I'm like that when I'm a hundred."

First of all he tried picking the lock. A thin small screwdriver bent into an L shape was inserted and twisted. An hour later the lock remained as fixed and permanent a part of her body as ever, but now covered in tell-tale scratches. Sally felt sure her husband would discover them and learn that she had been trying to escape.

David then suggested an electric drill, but Sally explained what the packaging had guaranteed and the plan was dropped.

That afternoon, with the lock unyielding, David used his fingers. By gently tickling around the fastening he was able to rouse her and slowly, erotically, make her come. It was beautiful.

Sally wanted the lock off. The more she rowed with Tony the more he laughed. She threatened to take him to the police and to court but he just ridiculed her threat: she would end up in the local and national papers, her predicament humiliatingly revealed to all.

Sally cried. Tony's sadism was growing. He would now make her say all sorts of terrible things before he would give her his quick fix. She even had to beg for it.

David's fingers, as wonderful as they were, could not be a substitute for his real member, certainly not since she had seen it: thick, stiff and excited. She longed for him.

Her release was the result of pure coincidence. Her best friend had locked herself out of her house. She asked Sally to cover for her while she took an hour off work to go to a locksmith to get a key.

"How can he know which key to give you?" inquired a mystified Sally.

Her friend revealed that she was always losing her keys, in fact it was a family failing; thus she had learned to make a note of the numbers of all her keys. Sometimes the number is on the lock, she added.

Sally immediately excused herself to go to the loo, checked and shrieked with joy. There was the number.

A visit to the locksmith, a story of a locked garden shed told by a blushing, stuttering girl, and a key was struck.

She phoned Tony and explained that she would be very late that night. And she was. David was everything she had ever missed: patient, imaginative, and always calmly, naturally, in control.

Her plan was formed during the drive home. With her pussy at long last free and open, she calmly reviewed the situation. Another lock was called for, with another key. It would be Tony's turn to beg, she decided. But he too would one day learn how to get a replacement key.

The do-it-yourself shop had the perfect answer.

Tony was a little perturbed that his randy wife no longer begged for sex; indeed, no longer mentioned it. Eventually he had to ask her for sex. She refused. He grew more passionate, more desperate. He learned the burning pain of frustration. After he had been made to ask nicely, Sally agreed, and a bewildered, desperate Tony went to get the key.

He returned to find her already in bed and immediately stripped down to his erection, falling over his trousers in his haste to pull them off.

His triumphant waving of the key desisted as soon as he saw Sally's new guardsman.

"A combination lock!" He mumbled.

Sally smiled coolly. "Now then," she began, "just remind me: how does a slut beg for sex?"

Subdued

Ken Davies

She was escorted down the long, austere hallway by two large black men, their muscles bulging, dressed only in skimpy loincloths. She was wearing just a thin, see-through white cloak, clasped at the neck. They held her, firmly but not harshly, by each elbow. They did not speak to her, but guided her to her destiny silently. It had been made clear to her that she should not speak.

At the end of the hallway, two large double doors awaited. One of the black men stepped ahead and pushed one of the doors open. They entered a large and opulently decorated study. Expensive-looking, leather-bound books lined floor-to-ceiling built-in bookcases. Fantastically colourful oil paintings were lit by small spotlights. Rich red tapestries matched the draperies covering the French windows.

As they walked into the room, she became aware of a semicircle of chairs facing her. Seven men, each expensively dressed, sat awaiting her. Some smoked, each had a drink in his hand; none spoke.

Midway into the room the black men stopped her, directly opposite the semi-circle of silent men. One of the seated men, handsome and tall, stubbed out his cigarette and put his drink down on a small mahogany side-table. He rose and approached her. Without a word, he reached for the clasp on her neck and undid it, letting the cloak slide to the floor. She stood before them in lustrous nakedness — tall, with long, shapely legs, an ample but firm set of hips, large, well-formed breasts.

The man before her slid a well-manicured forefinger along her neck, down her shoulder and across her chest. He cupped each of her large, big-nippled breasts in his hands. His hands were warm and the room was well heated by two large, crackling fireplaces, so she was not cold. His right hand slipped down, his forefinger circling and then probing her navel. Still he did not speak. His hand descended to tuft of curly blonde hair between her thighs. He twisted a bit of it between his fingers and stared into her eyes.

"My dear," he finally said. "You are our guest. You will be with us for some time, and for you time stopped when you entered this room. Resistance is pointless and foolish. These gentlemen will explore their desires at some length and these fellows, motioning towards the silent black men at her side, will assist us and you."

He circled around her, his hand stroking her hips. His fingers slipped down the crack between her firm buttocks and paused at her anus. His forefinger pushed gently at her puckered asshole, which tightened involuntarily. He did not persist but circled around her again. He glanced around at his associates and passed his fingers again through her pubic hair. "Gentlemen, let us proceed." He appeared to be the man in charge.

He stepped back from her, retrieved his drink and turned around to face her again. She was not particularly afraid, but was aware of her powerlessness. Motioning to the black men still at her side, the man said, "Her hood."

One of the black men stepped to a nearby cabinet and pulled from it a leather hood. He slipped this over her head and buckled it around her neck. There were holes for her nose and mouth, but she could see nothing.

The good-looking man, though now she could not see him, then commanded, "Hoist her up." One of the black men stepped to the side of the room and began cranking a winch-like apparatus she had not noticed before, when she could see. From the ceiling descended a set of not quite parallel bars. When it reached ground level, the black men silently pushed her to the floor. She sat while they placed the bar in front under her knees and strapped them to the bar, keeping her knees about three feet apart. Then they tied her wrists to the second bar. The restraints were well-padded and did not hurt.

When she was secured, one of the black men returned to the winch and began cranking. The bars slowly ascended, but she realised they were now uneven. Her knees rose higher than her wrists, leaving her bottom dropping and thrusting forward. Her large breasts splayed out slightly as she was hoisted up. She rose until her exposed pussy was about five feet from the carpet.

"Now, shave her," commanded the man in charge. One of the black men opened the cabinet and pulled out a shaving mug and razor. He soaped her pubic area, taking care to wipe the brush well into the crack of her ass as well. With a well-practised hand he deftly shaved her, taking good care not to nick her. Parting the cheeks of her buttocks, he also removed the downy hairs around her asshole and, after drying her with a soft towel, gently rubbed a fragrant and warm moisturising cream over the now bare skin.

The man in charge stepped forward to inspect the work. He placed his face just inches from the lips of her pussy and ran his forefinger gently over her now shaved womanhood. His other hand rose and, with thumb and forefinger, he pushed the lips gently apart, while his other hand cupped her buttocks. He peered into the pink recess and the gaze of the men behind him collectively focused on the same spot. Evidently pleased with the job, he stepped back. Turning to his fellows, he said, "Gentlemen, shall we dine?"

He motioned to one of the black men, who wheeled forward a small kitchen cart. He rolled back its cover to reveal a steam table. On it were a pot of rich yellow butter and a platter of steaming corn-on the cob.

"We'll have the corn," he said to one of the black men, then turned to the other and said, "Ready yourself." The second black man reached down and slipped off his loincloth. With one hand cupping his balls, he began to squeeze and pull on his prick. Almost instantly it sprang to height, an awesome arching tool about ten inches long and at least three inches across. Blood-engorged veins rippled along the shaft as he passed his hand slowly up and down its length. The other black man picked up the butter pot and, dipping a brush into it, started buttering up her pussy. He parted her lips and made sure he got plenty of the warm butter into her hole. He then picked up a basting tube with a rubber suction bulb on one end and filled it with butter. This he slowly inserted in her asshole, and then squeezed the bulb, filling her ass and its recesses with the golden liquid.

When he was done, the men rose silently from their chairs and approached the steam table. Each selected a cob of corn and dipped it in the butter pot. The man in charge approached her first.

Parting the lips of her pussy, he slowly inserted the narrow end of the corn cob. He pushed it gently into her, slowly twisting it. He paused and pulled it back, only to push it deeper on the next slow thrust. Finally its entire length was in her. Then he slowly withdrew it and stepped back. The man in charge smiled and started eating the corn. Each of the other men in turn inserted their corn cobs in her pussy, pausing between each entry for the black man to butter her again.

Meanwhile, the other black man continued slowly stroking his enormous prick. When all the men had finished and returned to their chairs, the man in charge wordlessly motioned to the waiting black man, who walked over to the winch and started lowering her towards the floor.

He stopped when she was about three feet above it and, making an adjustment in the apparatus, lifted her knees slightly higher, exposing her arsehole as her bottom pushed forward. He reached into the butter pot with his hand and cupped a handful of the warm butter over his prick, rubbing it up and down with his hand. Then, with one hand on her hip and the other guiding his shaft he slowly inserted the tip of his bulging prick into her asshole.

Throughout all this, she had been silent. The corn cobs had not hurt her and the men had all been slow and deliberate in their motions. But now she let out an involuntary yelp. Would this prick possibly fit up her behind? She of course couldn't see it, but she knew from the size of the black men that each must have an enormous weapon. She didn't know if even her pussy could possibly manage it.

The other black man brought over the butter pot and brushed her large tits all over. In pairs, the men left their chairs and came over, suckling on her nipples. Pulse racing, she grew more and more excited. The black cock in her ass pushed ever deeper, its master guiding it in and out in slow but ever-deeper thrusts.

She leaned back as far as she could in her trussed-up condition. As the black man thrust deeper and deeper, she rocked slowly back and forth, swinging from the ceiling. The rocking accentuated his thrusts, plunging his prick further and further into her. Finally, it was in up to the hilt. The black man paused, and a smile slowly spread across his face. He reached out with one hand pulling at one nipple and then the other. Both were taut with excitement. With his other hand, he started rubbing her clitoris, still buttery and moist from the corn.

Once again, an involuntary gasp passed her lips. As if on cue, the other black man made a further adjustment in the winch and lowered the bar holding her wrists. When her head was even with her hips, he stopped. Each of the men now rose from their chairs and unzipped their trousers. Each pulled out his already stiff prick and, stepping to the steam table, buttered up each one. The black man at the winch stepped over and gently turned her hooded head to the side. Each of the men stepped forward and in turn placed his prick in her mouth. She sucked on each, savouring the butter.

Meanwhile, the black man up her ass resumed his thrusts. Her rocking began again and the men taking turns at her mouth each swayed with her, keeping her mouth full.

As each was ready to come, he withdrew and the other black man stepped forward to grab each purpled dick with both hands. With each one, he locked a firm grip at the base of the prick and furiously frigged the head, causing each to erupt in a flurry of spewing semen. Each erupting geyser was directed at her chest and her tits were soon awash with a mixture of gooey white cum and the butter left from earlier.

The black man in her ass pounded on. Her breath came in short panting gasps. Her ass seemed afire as the black man rammed in and out. The other black man stepped to her side and began rubbing her clitoris. This too felt as if it were on fire. She felt the black prick inside her swell, and sensed it was about to explode.

Then, suddenly, the man in charged shouted "Stop!" Both black men instantly halted their endeavours. The black prick slowly withdrew. When its head finally emerged from her ass, the aching void seemed enormous and she passed a long and extremely wet fart.

Inside her mask, she blushed red. The man in charge chuckled lowly. "My dear," he said, "you have been very co-operative. But for that last indiscretion, further challenges await you."

"Let her down," he instructed the black men. One went to the winch and started cranking her down, while the other gathered her up in his arms. The other black man then came over and unfastened her wrists and removed the restraints on her legs. She swooned in the black man's arms and feared she would faint. The black man carried her to the far end of the enormous study while his mate drew back a curtain concealing a tall metal frame. From its top dangled two buckled straps. Her wrists were placed in the straps and she sagged, now suddenly exhausted.

"No, no, my dear," said the man in charge. "No rest for the wicked. On her toes," he added to the black men. One lifted her by the waist while the other shortened the straps until she was held standing on tiptoe.

"Now, I am afraid you must be punished for that embarrassing release," the man in charge said.

He had meanwhile undressed, and as he approached her his

prick stiffened in anticipation. He placed his right hand gently on her buttocks, gently fingering and squeezing the firm flesh. Then he drew it back suddenly and brought it down with a loud smack on her butt. She tried not to, but she let our a short yelp.

"No, no, my dear," the man in charge said, "you must enjoy it." He drew back his hand again and brought it down sharply on her other cheek. Two bright red hand marks glowed on her pale white flesh.

At the side of the metal frame stood a rack containing various implements. He looked over several before selecting a leather riding crop. Flexing it in his hands, he turned back to her. "Perhaps a little oil would help?" he asked. Not waiting for a reply, nor expecting one, he took a small bottle of oil and liberally smeared her butt with it. He raised the riding crop and then brought it down. Whack! She grunted but did not shout. Again his arm rose. Whack! A thin bead of sweat broke out on his brow and his prick grew even stiffer, its head glowing red.

Inside her hood, she clenched her teeth and tried to think of something else. But the riding crop had an uncanny ability to focus her attention. Her ass stung, more alive now than when that black prick was stuffed up her.

He paused in his work. The riding crop in his right hand, his left drifted down to his angry prick. Putting the crop back on the rack, he took the bottle of oil he had used on her ass, poured some in his hand and then over his aching member. He stepped back behind her, spread the cheeks of her ass, and slid his cock into her.

She was exquisitely aware of his loins pressing against her butt, her nerve endings picking out the hair on his thighs and surrounding the prick sliding up her backside.

He reached around her and grabbed a breast in each hand.

His fingers pulled and squeezed her nipples. As best she could on tiptoe, she arched, meeting his thrusts.

The sweat was now pouring from him. It ran down his stomach and onto her ass. Grabbing her by the waist, his strokes grew more insistent, more driven. A look of transfixed ecstasy gripped his features.

His mind no longer functioned; his whole being was concentrated in his driving prick. Suddenly he shouted, "Good God, I come!" and rammed his prick full inside her. She felt the hot, burning cum spurt into her ass. It felt as hot as lava. His prick jerked and heaved like a wild horse, pumping the fiery cum deep in her bowels. It felt to her as if there were gallons of it.

He remained deep inside her, impaling her, until he was spent. With a low groan, he finally pulled out and staggered back from the frame. His cock was still enormous but beginning to recede.

"Take her down," he ordered as he stumbled back to his chair, reaching for his drink.

The black men unstrapped her and led her away from the frame. She was led to a nearby divan and allowed to lie down. But then she felt her arms and legs spread-eagled and slipped into new straps, which were tightened and locked.

The man in charge gazed blankly into space. "Next," he said, and one of the other of the seven men rose and approached the divan, shedding clothes as he came. His stiffening prick rose, as if sniffing out its destination.

She waited, subdued.

L'Odalisque

J.D. Maguire

Claire raised an enquiring eyebrow over her coffee cup as she surveyed the pale features of her flatmate. "You look awful, Nicky. I didn't hear you come in, so it must have been late. I suppose you spent half the night fighting off Rob as usual." She sighed. "Perhaps you ought to let him have his wicked way; then you might get to bed at a reasonable hour."

They both worked at the claims office of Allied Mutual, and after a long search, had finally found a furnished apartment. That morning, they sat together in the small kitchen.

Nicola took a sip of coffee and shook her head, looking thoughtfully across at her friend, "Do I look odd, Claire?"

Claire shrugged. "Pale and interesting, I think it's called. Even so, there are plenty of girls who would be thrilled to look like you this morning, so don't worry about it — just get some earlier nights. That'll make you brighter in the mornings."

The other girl looked bemused. "But I did get to bed early — well, reasonably early. Rob dropped me off so that he could collect some relative at the station. Otherwise you could have been right. God, the hours I spend trying to get his hands out of my pants!"

Claire grinned. "It's not just his hands you have to keep out. Anyway, why so shattered this morning?"

Nicola bit her lip and looked at her. "I had this weird dream last night. It was so — so real. I can hardly begin to describe it. But when I woke up, I was totally — I don't know..."

Her friend put down her cup and looked interested. "Ooh, I love analysing other people's dreams! Do tell what it was about."

But Nicola went pink and pushed her chair back, rising from the table. "I can't remember," she stammered. "You know how it is with these things — the minute you open your eyes it's gone." She glanced at her watch. "Oh, look at the time! I'd better get under the shower, or we'll be late and I'll feel like death all day."

They had occupied the apartment for exactly a month, paying the rent to the estate agent, who had ushered them from room to room. The owner was a foreign gentleman now living in Spain. Two single bedrooms, kitchen, bathroom, and small but comfortable lounge. Furnishings tasteful without being opulent, and carpeted throughout.

'Suit two young single, personable females,' the ad had said.

"Beats me," Nicola had said as they surveyed the second bedroom. She turned and regarded the young man from the estate agent, who stood in the doorway twiddling the keys. "Why personable? If the owner is living permanently in Spain, why should he care what his tenants look like?"

He dragged his eyes from her shapely legs in the short skirt.

"It's a respectable neighbourhood — attractive clients for an attractive residence, I suppose. Anyway, those are his instructions."

"Do we fit the bill?" Claire raised her eyebrows.

The young man looked at them appreciatively and grinned. "I'll say!"

So they took the keys, handed over a cheque and moved in.

"First things first," said Nicola as they put their cases down. "Who gets which room?"

Both bedrooms were identically furnished and sited at the rear of the building. They looked out over a neat walled orchard with a curved path.

Nicola prodded the mattress and then sat on the edge of the bed. "OK, then. This one will suit me." The gilt frame of a picture hanging on the wall beside the divan bed caught her eye. She craned upwards from her sitting position. "Hey, take a look at this Claire."

Beneath the canvas and inset into the frame was the title — *'L'Odalisque.'* It depicted a woman reclining on a chaise longue. She was quite naked except for a filmy scrap of gossamer-like fabric that lay strategically over her hips. Above her stood a black man, wearing a turban and the briefest of white loincloths. The man, his skin obsidian and shining as though oiled, was bending towards the figure on the couch, holding a metal salver heaped with exotic fruits. The artist's brush brought the sheen on apple and pomegranate vividly to life.

The woman was raising a languid arm toward the proffered fruit, but her gaze was manifestly on the man rather than on what he was holding out to her. The musculature of his body was clearly defined beneath the jet-black skin, the biceps hard and bulging and the stomach flat and gleaming. It was the stark contrast of the soft, white contours of the woman and the brooding power of the figure towering over her that caught and held the girls' attention. The painting was skilfully executed and undeniably erotic, and Nicola looked away and shivered.

She looked at Claire wide-eyed, "Gosh, some picture! Your French is better than mine, Claire. What does the name mean?"

The other girl searched for her hazy French. *"L'Odalisque* — er, concubine. A woman in a harem, I think."

Nicola pointed at the woman and giggled. "Forbidden fruit — that's what she has on her mind, and I don't mean pomegranates!"

They laughed, went into the kitchen, made tea and then unpacked.

Temperamentally, as in almost every other respect, they were ideally suited as flatmates. They got on well together socially and at work. Both were in their early twenties, both were dark and attractive, and neither had heads that were easily turned by men, a considerable asset in an office where the opportunities for liaisons were countless.

Both girls got their share of sexual advances, but it was Nicola, with her long legs and svelte body, narrow-waisted and full-breasted, who was obliged to swat the hordes who descended as soon as she tucked her shapely limbs behind her desk.

Both were experienced without being promiscuous. Claire was free of entanglements at that time, licking her wounds and recovering from the perfidy of a man who had pretended to be available but was actually married — a fact betrayed by one of his colleagues in an unguarded moment. The man had had his face slapped, and Claire now bitterly regretted the undeniably exciting diversions she had found in his bed.

Nicola was currently seeing Rob, who worked in the Accidents section. A nice boy, she confided to Claire, "But I wouldn't like him to get the idea that I'm easy." She winked at Claire and stretched her marvellous legs. "It won't do him any harm to pant for a bit — then we'll see."

It was two days after Nicola's disturbed night that Claire suddenly woke and glanced at the clock beside her bed. The luminous numbers showed the time at a quarter past two in the morning. She was normally a sound sleeper, but something had roused her, and now she sat up and listened. And heard.

From the room next door — from Nicola's room — came the unmistakable sounds of lovemaking. Above the muted creaking of the bed came the throaty gasps of a woman in the arms of a lover. The gasps gave way to wild cries as the tempo increased, the creaking now becoming dull thuds as the bed took the straining of frenzied coupling.

Claire put her fingers in her ears to block out the noises, embarrassed at suddenly finding herself an eavesdropper, and then ducked her head beneath the bedclothes. She was puzzled too. They had both opted for an early night, and Nicola had been the first to go to the bathroom before saying goodnight. Why bother to pretend to go to bed, and then smuggle Rob upstairs? It wasn't necessary. They were both broadminded, for heaven's sake!

Then another thought occurred. Perhaps it was someone other than Rob. But if so, who? They had no secrets from each other. She turned over irritably, determined to speak to Nicola the next morning. Half an hour later, when she poked her head out, there was silence once more. She sighed and slept.

Claire was brushing her teeth when Nicola stepped out of the shower cubicle. She reached for a towel and wrapped it around her head. Claire opened her mouth to speak, looked at her friend's body and jumped. The beads of water on Nicola's naked flesh magnified the lividity that stood out on her breasts and thighs – angry looking smudges where a lover's hands and mouth had pressed too urgently in the transports of love.

Claire put down her toothbrush and pointed. "I hope you didn't leave *him* unmarked," she said dryly.

Nicola looked down and stared as if she was seeing the blemishes for the first time, then looked blankly back at her friend. "Leave *who* unmarked?"

"Rob, of course — or whoever you took to bed with you last night." She put her hands on her hips. "Look, Nicky, it doesn't make any difference to me, you should know that. You don't have to make a secret of having a man in your bed. Just let me know in future; I'll get some ear plugs."

"But I *didn't* have a man in my bed." Nicola's lip trembled, and she reached for a towel and dabbed slowly at her face. "I swear to you. I went to bed before you — and alone."

Claire looked at her, baffled. "What about those marks then? And what about the noises coming from your room last night? You were having an orgy in there, for heaven's sake!"

"I swear to you, Claire — there was no one in my room last night. As for the marks, I must have bumped into something — I hadn't noticed until now." She held the towel to her face. "God, but I did have another dream last night." Her whole body shook at the recollection, and she took hold of herself. "Look, I'd better get dressed."

Claire wiped the steam from the mirror and looked at her reflection. *One* of them was behaving oddly. Could she have imagined the incident? It was all very perplexing. She shook her head, slipped off her robe and stepped under the shower.

That evening Claire switched off the television and turned to Nicola, who sat in the chair opposite, her long legs tucked beneath her.

"OK, Nicky, I believe you. You didn't have Rob or anyone else in bed with you last night, and you got those marks by bumping into something — but what I heard last night were the sounds of someone being bonked. You explain it, because I can't."

Nicola gazed across at her for a long moment before answering. "All right, but what I tell you is the truth. Will you believe that?"

Claire looked at her solemn face and wide eyes. "Of course," she murmured.

Nicola's second dream had been identical to the first. She had woken from a deep sleep with the scent of something like incense in her room. Stirring, she opened her eyes and found herself lying on the crimson couch featured in the painting that hung above her bed. Then she saw the dark figure of the man leaning over her, bearing the fruit-laden tray, ebony muscles gleaming.

Simultaneously she became aware of two things. Like the woman in the painting, she was both naked and sexually aroused. Her eyes moved from the man to her breasts, and she was startled to see their tips swollen and erect, craning upwards and towards him. She was thankful that at least her loins were draped in the fragment of silk, but when she looked down it was gone, and she was bare to his gaze.

It was only a dream, but she wanted to move, to conceal her flesh from the hunger that lurked behind the man's burning gaze. But she found herself paralysed — like a rabbit caught and transfixed in the beam of an oncoming car.

As if in slow motion he moved, and now her dream took on new, terrifying proportions. He placed the tray on a low table and stood upright before her, his body assuming the dimensions of a giant. Lying there, supine and unable to move, her heart beat wildly and she saw the rapid rise and fall of her breasts.

Slowly and unhurriedly his hands moved to the meagre scrap of cloth that girded his hips, and it came away, falling to the floor. Now she saw his phallus, long and oiled and, like the rest of his body, erect and pulsing.

She gazed, repelled but unutterably aroused as he came forward, lips parted and strong white teeth gleaming, to mount her, his large hands parting her thighs. As he began to penetrate her she cried out with mingled pain and pleasure and found herself able to move, able to clasp the broad shoulders that towered over her. His member was feverishly hot, but the skin beneath her clutching fingers was as cold as polished marble, and as odourless. It was like being violated by a statue, but as the speed of his thrusts accelerated she was overwhelmed by the most intense orgasms she had ever known, until at last he quivered and ejaculated deep inside her, his seed a burning flood.

"I must have passed out then," Nicola murmured, "because when I woke up I was in my bed feeling cold, with all the clothes on the floor." She shook her head. "Having a dream like that once can be explained logically, I suppose, but twice..."

"It sounds more like a nightmare than anything else," commented Claire doubtfully. "Look, I don't want to sound prurient or anything, but couldn't those dreams — or nightmares — be the result of — well, frustration. You're a healthy girl with healthy appetites; perhaps you've been fighting off Rob for too long, and now your libido has expressed itself while you're asleep."

"So your suggestion is that I let Rob get his leg over — is that it?"

Claire shrugged. "It's worth a try, but in the meantime why don't we change rooms for a while — or take that bloody picture down: out of sight, out of mind!"

Nicola shook her head. "I expect you're right. I *am* uptight about Rob, but I can't do anything about him for the next week. He's away on a course until the weekend. But there's something else I haven't mentioned. During the dreams, I had the feeling that everything was being watched by someone — an unseen audience. In a way it was the worst part, as if I was being used to put on a show for someone." She shuddered at the thought.

"Are you sure you don't want to change rooms?"

Nicola got up and shook her head. "No, I won't give in to a dream. But have you still got those sleeping pills?"

Seven uneventful nights later, Nicola stretched and yawned. "I'm off to bed for an early night. I'm seeing Rob tomorrow — and who knows?" They both laughed, and soon the apartment was in darkness.

Claire stumbled from her bed, snapped on the light and threw her robe over her shoulders, hurrying towards the other room, from where the cries of her friend had brought her bolt upright in bed. Throwing Nicola's door wide, she fumbled for the light switch.

She lay there utterly naked, her body glistening with perspiration, thighs spread and drawn up to her chest, hips jerking upwards spasmodically, her hands defensively gripping the shoulders of some unseen partner and her eyes fixed in horror at an empty cane chair that stood a few feet from the bed.

Unnerved by the ghastly tableau, Claire stood in the doorway for a few seconds, gathered herself and flew to the bedside, taking her friend by the shoulders and shaking her. As she bent over it seemed to her that she passed through a current of cold air that chilled her to the bone, and the faint whiff of burning incense drifted across her nostrils.

As Claire clutched her, Nicola stiffened abruptly, held her breath and then cried out in the throes of some unimaginable ecstasy. Then it passed. Her limbs slithered down the bed and she turned her head, seeing her friend for the first time.

Then, recalling what had happened, she shuddered, threw her arms around Claire and began to weep, racked by guilt at the memory of how her body had responded. "I saw him," she sobbed. "I saw him." She pointed to the chair. "He was sitting there watching me — watching us, gloating at what was happening." Claire held her at arm's length. "Saw who? Who was sitting there?"

Nicola used the edge of her sheet to wipe her eyes. "He was old, dressed in a white suit and shirt open at the collar. Long grey hair down to his shoulders. And a wart or something on his cheek. He was leaning forward on a walking stick — and there was a gold ring on the little finger of his right hand with a red stone set into it."

Claire stared at her. "Wait here," she said and ran from the room, reappearing with a small black and white photograph in her hands. "Look at this!" she said grimly.

"My God, it's the man in my dream! Look! That's the same ring!" She looked at Claire in disbelief. "Where did you find it?"

"It was underneath the paper lining in the chest of drawers. I meant to show it to you. I think it's the guy who owns this apartment — the one who lives abroad. Now take a closer look at that picture."

Nicola bent over the photograph once more and gasped. The elderly man was looking into the lens with a kindly smile, but he was sitting in a high backed cane chair, and behind him hung the portrait of the servant and concubine. But it was the malevolence in the eyes that gripped her. She shook her head and stared at Claire, baffled. "I don't understand," she said.

Claire got up. Her face was grim. "Neither do I, but I'm not waiting for an explanation. Get dressed, Nicky. I'll make some tea, but as soon as it's light we're leaving this place — bag and baggage!"

"Where will we go?"

Claire stopped on her way out of the room. "Anywhere — as long as it's miles from here."

At the estate agents' office, Mike Burridge looked at the screen, gave a whistle, and turned to his secretary. "It's crazy! That apartment in Charteris Road has had more tenants in the last year than I've had hot dinners." He counted. "Six lettings in less than twelve months." He shrugged. "Oh well, there are plenty more girls looking for a place like that. Put out the ads again, will you, please, Julie?"

Foolishness

Mike Perkins

He sat opposite his wife in the self-service café, idly watching the queue while she wrote postcards to their married children. On holiday in Dorset for the sixth successive year, he was feeling bored and aware that the years were slipping by.

He debated whether another biscuit would he catastrophic to his waistline. As he looked up at the price list on the wall, he saw the youngster make for a table in the corner.

His pulse rate increased as his eyes registered the vision. Young, probably no more than sixteen, seventeen at the most. Elfin-faced, she glowed with the bloom of youth. Long golden curls hung down past her shoulders, drawn back to expose the ears, and a pair of extrovert pendant earrings dangled from dainty lobes. She wore no obvious make-up except a trace of shadow above the big blue orbs that were her eyes.

He watched with fascination as she sipped cola through a

straw, emphasising the natural pout of her mouth. Dressed in a loose mauve cheesecloth shirt and tight denim jeans, she was an absolute picture. Emotions, long dormant, began to stir as he fantasised about how she'd look without clothes. He guessed she'd have well-shaped breasts above her tiny waist.

He adjusted his position to take the pressure off the erection beginning to throb between his legs, but carried on watching, entranced by her natural beauty and enjoying the erotic sensations rippling along his shaft as he clenched the muscles in his groin. He noticed that she kept looking around the room like a startled gazelle, as if uncomfortable at being alone. Their eyes locked for a brief second and he smiled before she looked away.

His reverie was broken when his wife told him she'd finished and passed him the cards to read, then said that they must go and buy stamps.

He stood outside the Post Office while his wife queued at the counter, and suddenly the youngster was beside him. "I saw the way you were looking at me," she whispered urgently. "If you want me, be in the lay-by outside Scott's campsite at seven this evening."

He opened his mouth in surprise, but she'd gone before he could think of a response.

They spent the rest of the day on the sea front, admiring the formal flower beds and listening to the music at the bandstand. But all the while he was preoccupied with the girl and her invitation.

Was she really offering herself to him? Should he go to meet her? Was it fair to go sniffing around such a gorgeous young girl at his age, especially since his wife had forgiven his last misdemeanour a few years ago?

Hell, it's been a long time since I've broken fresh ground, he decided finally. There's no way I should pass up this chance, if

I can get away with it.

After their evening meal in the caravan, he carefully manipulated his wife. "What do you feel like doing?" he asked innocently. "The weather's so nice, I feel like going out again."

"Don't be silly," she replied. "It's Coronation Street tonight, then that new serial. Can't miss that!"

"I'm fed up with watching telly every night," he whinged. "I feel like doing something different."

"You do what you like," she snapped, "but I'm watching television."

"You wouldn't mind if I went out for a mooch around on my own?"

"No, why should I?" she asked.

Not sure whether the girl's invitation had been genuine, but excited nevertheless, he parked the car up the road from the lay-by and walked to the appointed meeting place.

She was waiting, dressed exactly as before except that her feet were bare.

"You came, then. I thought you would," she greeted him with a fetching grin. "I was pretty sure you fancied me."

"Well, you are very attractive..." he mumbled, her direct approach making him feel self-conscious. "I can't imagine how any red-blooded man could resist you."

"Thanks," she smiled, "but don't expect too much from me; I'm not used to doing this sort of thing. Come on, follow me."

She led him a few yards to a small igloo tent. When they were both inside, she crouched and removed her shirt and jeans. Naked except for a tiny pair of briefs, she looked up at him with those luminous orbs.

"You will pay?"

"Of course," he agreed as his eyes consumed her youthful body. "How much?"

"I don't know the going rate," she said, pouting slightly. "I've never done this before. I lost my purse this morning and this is the only way I can afford to stay for the rest of my holiday. Let's say twenty pounds?"

"That's all right," he agreed, excited by the sight of her slim thighs, but slightly dejected by her story. "I'll help you anyway, if you don't want to have sex..."

"No; nobody should get something for nothing. I need the money, so it's a fair swap." She looked at the bulge in his trousers. "Have you got a condom?"

"No, I'm afraid not," he admitted, suddenly afraid her body was about to be denied him after all.

"Then I think it's normal to charge double if you want to go all the way. Am I worth forty pounds?"

He agreed immediately, and fumbled for the notes while she bent to remove her pants.

Blood rushed to his head and his heart hammered as he realised he really was going to be allowed to have his way with this wisp of a girl, so much younger than his own children. He gazed at her small, firm breasts, narrow waist, flat belly with a slightly proud button, and slender thighs, parted so that he caught a glimpse of her intimate slit, surrounded by fair hair.

Her figure was perfect. He'd known a few young bodies in his time, but none that excited him to the pitch he now felt as he anticipated how she'd feel beneath him.

His rod throbbed beneath his trousers as he watched her spread-eagle herself on a sleeping bag. He gazed at the open lips below her mound, scarcely able to breathe as excitement pounded to the very core of his body.

"Come on, then," she instructed impatiently, opening her legs and fingering her groin.

He shed his clothes quickly and fell down beside her. He

kissed each of her breasts, the centre of her belly and her pubic mound. His mouth lingered at her fleshy brim as he inhaled the sweet smell of her sex. His hands trembled as they touched her satiny skin. He wanted to devour her.

Fighting an urge to ravish her, he made a conscious decision to pleasure her before surrendering to his own craving. He drooled as his fingers slipped over her thigh towards the gate of heaven, seeking to stimulate the hard little button that he knew lurked within. He concentrated on the downy fair hair on her outstretched arms as he fought to control himself.

"Stop mucking about," she whispered. "Just give it to me straight. I don't want any fancy stuff my first time."

"First time!" The words burnt into his consciousness. She'd already said it was the first time she had sold herself, but was she suggesting he was about to deflower a virgin? The thought excited him beyond reason as he obeyed, climbed between her legs and probed for her honeypot with his pulsating organ. Her touch was like an electric shock as she reached down and guided him in with her fingers.

It was tight, far tighter than he remembered adolescent cunts could be. Her muscles twitched, clenched and rippled along his cock as he fought to drive it in. He pushed harder and slipped in all the way, bouncing hard against her mound. He withdrew slightly and pushed again. There was no resistance, her natural lubrication making a slight slurping sound as he pumped back and forth.

She began to undulate her hips, picking up the rhythm of his thrusts. Looking down at her, he saw her pensively sucking her bottom lip before their eyes met. She smiled, clenched the muscles at her groin even more tightly to grip his twitching shaft, and milked him as he shot his pent-up load into her warm cavern.

They laid still for a few seconds before she pushed him off. "All right, you've had what you came for," she sniffed, her eyes glistening with tears. "Now get dressed and bugger off."

Her abruptness brought him back to earth with a bump. What had he done?

Ashamed, he dressed quickly, dropped an additional twenty-pound note beside the naked girl, and fled. He sat in his car for five minutes, filled with remorse, and started to worry. Perhaps he shouldn't have left so quickly? She was obviously upset. Maybe he ought to go back and make sure she'd recovered?

He crept behind a bush opposite the tent. She was dressed and sitting outside with a youth. He watched as she handed over the money. They exchanged a brief kiss, then the boy looked at his watch and disappeared into the woods.

As he crouched down, the girl passed close to him as she made for the lay-by. He followed, staying out of sight, and saw her walk up to a parked car.

Holding his breath, he strained to hear the conversation. "You came, then. I thought you would. I was pretty sure you fancied me..."

Death & Seduction

Catherine Sellars

Gabriel's body cuts through the heat curtain dividing street from arcade. For a moment external and internal are indistinguishable, until all the sounds and scents of the exterior are sucked back into their rightful place.

The drone and chime of conversation and cutlery fill the dome above her, recalling memories of tastes and sensations that become more exquisite with each recollection. Gabriel's eyes become adjusted to the warm light and focus on the faces of shoppers, rendered beautiful by the carefully created glow. They stroll in calm contentment, with expressions of reverence and awe, complimenting and admiring, more like an audience at a great exhibition than consumers in a mall.

Through the delicately wrought iron and engraved glass, Gabriel spies her victim. She eyes her prey, wets her lips and crosses the expanse of jewelled mosaic like a society courtesan making a path through a crowded ballroom to her potential Prince.

The prey, a young man with a touch too much red in his cheeks and his locks too brassy to be those of a classic beauty, is comely enough nevertheless. Track-suited and chain-smoking, he slouches against the wooden-fronted candle shop, squat shape with a halo of flickering flames. He has as little sense of style as he has of his impending doom.

Gabriel uses her clipboard like an antique fan. The delicate movements of a courtly ritual long dead tug unconsciously at the cultural memory of the youth, for he smiles and bows his head on cue, saying all the right things at all the right moments. Each flutter and tilt of the clipboard beckon him closer to his destruction.

A little polite conversation gives way to a few simple questions concerning his habits as a consumer. Gabriel once again employs her clipboard as a fan, but this time in its more conventional fashion, for she grows warm with anticipation of coming pleasure. The format of the questionnaire, you see, and her promises of a reward at its completion are cunningly designed to appeal to all the vices in man, playing on the human frailties of laziness, greed and lust with expert skill, and coaxing white lies from his lips in defence of his frail ego.

Flattered into a sense of stupid pride at his ability to recognise brands of toothpaste by their logo, his good taste in cars and the amount of alcohol-free lager he might consume in a month, the young man's defences begin to crumble. Vanity parades his vices in an unwitting confession of guilt.

Then comes the invitation, and a promise that he might discover something to his advantage or receive his reward should he follow her. Greed and lust chain him to her, and Gabriel triumphantly trots her mortal specimen out of the centre, through the crowds of consumers and into the night.

The city's floodlights glow into life at the perfect moment to illuminate the lowering heavens and turn the sudden squall into a crystal light show. Immediately the dull pavement becomes a dark mirror to the cityscape. At this impressive piece of celestial stage management, Gabriel picks up the skirts of her coat, deeply inhales the ozone-charged air and flies along the sparkling streets homeward to the Merchant City, her captive in morbid pursuit. The setting is ideal and the atmosphere inspiring, but totally lost on the unsuspecting victim, whose whole being is now focused on the body of his seducer. Nights like this give meaning to her existence, for on a night like this her true genius can reveal itself and her powers of creative destruction flourish.

Entering the hallway of her home, Gabriel sways free of her sable coat. The shock of metal heels on marble is muffled by the shuffle of his rubber-soled Reeboks as the sounds merge high up above the picture rail. A long bronze lady on an onyx plinth obligingly raises a globe of light to the crazed and ancient mirror, her back arched in an ecstasy of lunar worship. Gabriel's sepia-toned reflection, a Theda Bara in this amber glow, gazes out at the breathless youth on the doormat. As the last sounds of their entrance die away, the muted sounds of a tragic melody filter from the room ahead, Gershwin or Porter, Puccini or Rachmaninov — an irresistible and passionate keening.

Gabriel glides down the long corridor past fatal beauties with sailors entwined in their hair and disarmed knights at their feet: mermaids and sirens and *belles dames sans merci*. The wan faces of their victims, tragic and lovely, gaze down from the captivity of their picture frames at the unsuspecting youth. Blind with lust and ignorant in his certainty, he takes no heed of their silent warning. Water nymphs lure Hylas to his airless end, while Morgan le Fay eternally bewitches, but they perform their terrible function unrecognised. The young man does not even glance at them.

Gabriel, coatless, is dressed to kill. Her body is a metronome that swings hypnotically before him to the throb of the melancholy music, accompanied by the murmur of velvet on silk as her skirts sigh against her stockings. Gabriel leads the man along the endless corridor of panels and paintings, exhaling myrrh and spices and charging the air with rich scents and ozone. She leaves a trail of musk that the man must follow. At last they reach the door at the corridor's end. Gabriel glides a hand over her waist and hips and waves the prey into her room. She strolls in behind him, eager to embark on her fatal labours.

The light in the room is cool silver and blue. The stormy night, viewed in panorama through the room's enormous windows, is huge and indigo. Despite the casements flung wide, the air is heavy with the scent of three great lilies.

Gabriel takes a liquor glass, silver vines entwining its stem, and pours a slick of noxious liquid into it. It shines with emerald light. The stupid youth takes the glass without a question, bewitched by the ruby, amethyst and jet that are her lips, eyes and hair. As he sips the poison and inhales its fumes, he does not notice its bitter taste, for his senses are dazzled into dullness. Gabriel looks on in satisfaction and drapes herself in ecstasy over the vast blue velvet sofa.

The youth falls helpless into her arms and she absorbs all the life from him, drinking in his strength and watching all that disgusted her seep slowly away. At last he is no longer an uncouth sinner. He has become her object. An object with more potential than she ever imagined on first setting eyes on his rough, unrefined form. He will make a most beautiful corpse, and his death will be magnificent.

She carries the senseless young man into a high-ceilinged bathroom of dolphins and sea nymphs and, despite his weight, glides effortlessly over the floor. She undresses him slowly and carefully, and places his limp, damp clothes in the fire of the polished copper boiler. They hiss disagreement before bursting into flames. Gabriel then takes a gleaming silver blade from the bathroom cabinet, a bottle of peroxide, some scissors, scented oils, a razor, soap and a shaving brush, and lines them up on the shelf beside the great cast-iron bath. While she runs the water she cuts the young man's hair into a tousled cap of curls. She then undresses and steps into the steaming, scented water with her victim in her arms.

Gabriel washes away all traces of his mortal life — the stale stench of cheap deodorant and sweat, and the rancid smell of smoke in his hair. Unable to move or speak, only the look of terror in the dying man's eyes show that he has any awareness of his situation. Gabriel runs her hands over the hard muscle and taut sinews, stroking and massaging his malleable form, then shaves his entire body. She applies the peroxide to his brassy locks and, while she waits for it to take effect, she glides the silver blade across each wrist and lies back to watch her terrible bath turn red with the blood of her victim. The life pours out of him and she captures a little of it in a small glass vial. He labours to breathe his last, succumbing to the poison and the loss of blood. Gabriel feels an involuntary spasm in the walls of her stomach as he releases his final sigh. She rinses the chemicals from his now silver hair, and after wrapping his body in great warm towels she moisturises the smooth, white skin.

Gabriel dresses the beautiful corpse in a pure silk shirt, voluptuous in the generosity of its cut, and a pair of high-waisted trousers of the finest fabric. She applies kohl to his lids, mascara to his lashes and a wine-coloured stain to his lips. She carries her beautiful work out of her room, along the endless corridor and out into the city. In her pocket is the vial of blood and beneath her coat are white narcissus and orchids. She passes unhindered through the sleeping city and enters its cultivated parkland. The storm is over, the night is still, crisp and clear. A huge pewter moon illumines a dark sapphire sky and lights the way to the final resting place.

Gabriel lays him gently in the frozen fountain at the centre of the botanical gardens. In a pose of carefully engineered disarray, his head rests casually on one arm, the limbs draped over the marble, everything arranged to the greatest aesthetic effect. Only one task remains. She plunges the gorgeous blade into the heart of the dead man, between the folds of his shirt. She arranges the narcissus and orchids about his body, placing one in his dangling fingers and others around his shining hair and at his feet.

She drips a little of the contents of the vial around the bloodless wound in his chest, perfectly choreographing the trickle of blood so that it curves delicately over the line of his pectorals. She places a single drop at the corner of his burgundy lips and delicately strokes a wisp of platinum hair from his heavy blue lids. She lingers a moment to gaze at her work, gleaming white against the moonlight, the perfect man reclining on a crystal throne, shimmering with purity, untainted by life, released from bestiality for a brief moment, before the sun rises, melts the fountain and sets the machinery of decay into motion.

Gabriel records the scene in her memory and disappears back into the city.

The Depilator

Bill Campbell

He felt his interest rising. He tried to imagine what she looked like. Was the face ever a guide to what lay below? His experience to date was hardly large, but he knew that the beauty of the vulva was quite independent of the facial impression. He went over to check his tools. Should he take them with him, on the off-chance that she might agree straight away? Or would it be presumptuous? He preferred to work from home, in any case; his best results were always achieved in familiar surroundings with predictable light, comfortable access and just the right temperature of water. Would she have the necessary towels and cloths? Would the furniture present her at the right angle? Would she be comfortable? Anyway, he had to meet her first before a decision could he made. He completed his last arrangements, then headed off for the gallery where they'd arranged to meet at an exhibition of Orta nudes.

He saw her immediately. A burst of excitement shot through him. A redhead! He'd never had that privilege before. He knew it was her; the slight uncertainty as she stood in front of the drawing, itself showing a proud dominant mons, clean of disfiguring hair, thrust forward in a provocatively sexual pose. He wondered if Orta had shaved it himself before lifting a brush. Had it still that soft dampness that slowly dissolved into taut skin, as his charcoal slewed across the paper? He looked up again. She was now looking distinctly edgy. She probably thought he wasn't coming, that she was a damn fool for coming this far, it had to be a hoax, no one seriously did this kind of thing.

He walked beside her. He took a breath, and spoke.

"Fine picture. It's nice to see such accuracy."

She turned suddenly. She was obviously thinking how to find out if the man standing beside her was the one she expected.

"Er, yes. It's, um, interesting that the, er, the pudenda are so prominent."

He picked up on the lead. "I'm Jones."

"Oh, good." She looked lost.

"Shall we sit down?"

"All right." They sat in front of an Orta self-portrait, his naked penis sealed in red.

"Why do you want to use my service, if you don't mind me asking?"

"It just seems the right thing to do. I've heard it improves sensation, it's certainly more hygienic. Something different. Quite a few girlfriends have done it. I wear a high-waist swimsuit, too, and it's difficult to achieve a clean line."

"Why not do it yourself, or get your lover to do it? Why a stranger like me?"

"I don't know. I don't really enjoy doing it to myself. I'm not in a relationship at the moment, either. It just seems right to get a specialist."

She dried up, and looked uncomfortable. Jones decided to take the initiative.

"Well, if you're happy to do so, I have everything ready at my studio."

"Studio?"

"Why not? I'm as much an artist in my own way as Orta." She grinned at that.

They moved off, and took her car to Jones' house. They made polite conversation in the car as Jones directed her; the weather, the exhibition they had just seen. Jones led her into the hall and took her coat.

"Please come into the studio," he said.

She followed him through. She was struck by the utilitarian surroundings, although the detail was lavish. A large leather couch formed the centrepiece to the room. A small trolley, clearly oak and beautifully finished, stood beside it. A Persian carpet covered the floor. Fine paintings filled the walls, principally nudes; she recognised a Botticelli and perhaps a Renoir. A door, ajar, led off into what appeared to be a bathroom. Incongruously, a clearly expensive Italian hi-tech halogen lamp dominated at the end of the couch. Jones broke into her thoughts.

"There's a few arrangements for me to make. Would you like to get ready? I'd like you to wash; it helps to soften the hair. There's a bidet in the room through there. You'll find a gown behind the door, if you'd like to put that on after you've removed your underclothes. When you feel ready, if you could just come through?"

She walked in and did as he asked. There was a hanger and

a shelf for her clothes. She removed her outer clothes, hung them up, slipped off her panties, and debated about whether to remove the bra as well. After a second's thought she unclipped it and placed it on the shelf. She ran the bidet, and warmed it through until it felt comfortable She straddled it, sat down, and enjoyed the feel of the warm water lapping against her. She reached for the soap, noted that it was the unscented, pure variety, and slowly worked round the vulva and up over the mons. She replaced the soap, then ran away the water and used the central fountain to wash away the suds. She misjudged the tap and the first gush penetrated her; the shock surprised her and she quickly closed the tap. She suddenly realised that she was becoming aroused; her outer lips were filling and parting. She tried again with the fountain and got it just right this time. She reached for a towel from the rail beside her, raised herself from the bowl and slowly towelled herself dry, gently dabbing rather than rubbing, noting that not all the moisture she dried away came from the tap. She put on the gown and the mules she found underneath it, and walked back into the studio.

She saw Jones adjusting something in a drawer in the trolley. Two porcelain bowls and linen had appeared on top of it. Large towels covered the couch. He turned to face her.

"Oh, fine. Was everything all right for you?"

She nodded.

"Please sit down on the end of the couch. That's it, about halfway down. Now, swing your legs over the end. Lovely. Would you like a pillow under your head? Fine. Now, would you like to open your legs?"

She felt her pulse rate rising crazily. What on earth was she doing here? What crazy risk was she running? She gripped the sides of the couch and thought about rushing for the door.

Jones could sense her apprehension.

"Please don't worry," he said. "Just relax and enjoy this."

His voice had a soothing quality that took the edge off her fear. She relaxed slightly. Jones' hands slowly separated her legs and bent them at the knee. She felt a cool draught across her vulva. Then a sharp buzzing distracted her. She looked down. Jones was resting between her legs, concentrating hard on his hand as it moved across her thatch with a small electric clipper. She watched, fascinated as the ginger hair fell away from the cutters into an orange ball. Jones cleared that and moved on to another track. She began to relax.

Jones breathed hard as he concentrated on keeping the clippers just above the flesh. Any higher, and the razor to follow would soon clog. Lower, and he might risk catching the skin. He moved the blades from right to left across the mons, cutting a clear swathe each time. He was fascinated by the ginger hair that rolled up; he'd never seen this colour before, and it had a peculiar springiness all of its own. He was amazed to see freckles appearing behind the clipper, and the most beautiful white skin, almost translucent, tracking across the delta. He moved down further to the junction of the lips, clearing the cut hair section by section to a waiting howl. He tut-tutted as he reached the obviously amateur attempts at clearing hair by the leg crease; the inflamed follicles told their own story. The woman clearly heard him, and her eyes flickered as she understood his survey. He moved back for a second as he completed the last track, and admired the glory of what lay before him. He looked at the woman, and he saw what almost seemed a look of anticipation in her eyes. She was calm now, and stared intently at his efforts.

He now moved down to the lips. This, now, was where all his skill was needed. He trimmed away down each side of the outer lips, holding his breath as he concentrated intently on staying clear of the delicate flesh peeping through the jungle of hair. Gradually the cuttings were swept clear, and he slowed down to target his attention on difficult areas. The woman sensed his efforts, and moved her legs further apart to ease the task. He now had to lift the outer lips proud, to complete that section, and for the first time he had to touch her vulva. He inserted his gloved finger between the inner and outer lip, and he felt a surge run through the woman as he touched her. He was now aware of her excitement, and noted that her vagina was beginning to open, showing shell-pink and moist as his fingers moved down the lip one side at a time.

Finishing his first task, he pulled back to prepare the razor.

"Are you feeling all right? I haven't hurt you at all? Are you comfortable? Not cold, are you?"

The response was something close to a purr. Her eyes had a clear gleam, and her lips were slightly parted. He recognised the signs, and moved over to his drawer. He soaked a small towel in hot water, squeezed it dry, checked the temperature carefully, then applied it to her mons and vulva. The woman squirmed, then relaxed. She exhaled with a satisfied sigh. He left the towel for a few more seconds, then prepared a shaving gel, chosen after much experimentation. He smoothed it into the hair area, just tracing the tip of the outer lips while avoiding the inner softness.

As soon as he'd finished, he wiped his hands, then broke off the cover of the mirror and started to smooth off the clipped hairs, rinsing the blade in the other bowl after each run. Gradually the skin lay clear, denuded of shade, lying moist and plump. He finished the mons, and moved to the downy covering on the outer lips. Biting his tongue in concentration, oblivious now to the world outside the edge of the razor, he moved down to the outer lip with supreme care, responding to every undulation in the skin, keeping the razor moving to avoid the chance of a stall and thus the possibility of a nick. For that was the trademark of the amateur, the battlefield of nicks and razor burn, the islands of lost hairs. He was dimly aware that now her outer lips had spread wide, the inner lips had blossomed open, her clitoris stood proud and her vagina almost dripped with obvious arousal, the wetness glistening across the opening and the juices dripping down the perineum and mixing with the foam.

He continued moving the razor down towards her anus, dimly visible in the folds of the gown lying under her. He always found the puckered brown skin faintly distasteful, and stopped the razor short, leaving the ruched orifice still framed with its auburn collar. The perfection lay in the vulva, in its fineness, and almost gossamer parchment; the workmanlike anus distracted from the ideal, and was best left alone. Worse, to effectively clear it he would have to turn the woman on her stomach, an operation whose inelegance he shuddered at; the loss of dignity as she posed like an animal would destroy the aesthetics of the whole operation. So he moved up again, and quickly and smoothly retouched an area or two which still seemed to have a trace of hair. He then put down the razor, made up another hot towel, and gently wiped away all traces of the gel, smoothing the skin. As he lifted the towel clear, a skein of vulval juice stretched across, then fell away. The woman was now breathing fairly deeply, eyes heavy lidded, the ghost of a smile on her face.

The final act. He took some pure talcum, and sprinkled it finely and sparsely over the shaven areas. He then rolled off his gloves, and smoothed in the talc with his bare fingers, lingering in the edge of the lips, then finally passing both hands in from the thigh, pressing in the outer lips, moving up from the mons, then lifting them clear. He moved back, and bowed his head, rested his hands and breathed deeply.

He had finished. After a few seconds, he lifted his eyes, and took in the glory of his handiwork. Framed by her thighs, the engorged lips spread each side of the vagina, now fully open. The inner labia fluttered against the outer, wavy and shiny. As his eyes moved up he saw the labia joined at the vestibule, then they disappeared in the infinite parallax of the smooth and curving mons, where a couple of drops of moisture shone like diamonds on a counterpane. It was indeed perfect. His eyes met the woman's. In them he read the full understanding of what he had achieved. She slowly rear anged herself, sat up on the edge of the couch, and wordlessly returned to the bathroom.

When she returned, dressed as she had arrived, but now with an indefinable knowledge in her glance and movement, she found Jones still lost in contemplation of that perfect vista, and she knew that as she walked out the door, no further word having been uttered, that there would be no demand for payment; Jones had received his remuneration in full.

Lampyris Noctiluca

Sam Barford

It would be inaccurate to say that Gabriela's cunt glowed in the dark. The effect, when she raised her skirt in the carefully darkened room, removed her knickers and opened her legs, was rather of some powerful invisible light source, angled and focused so that her outer labia exactly bounded the lit area. There was, of course, no such light source, and the hushed spectators were as incapable of explaining the phenomenon as they were awed and aroused by the sight of it. The awe was marginally stronger than the arousal: no one had ever tried to touch her at one of these sessions, until the night I took Eduardo.

If the miraculous light was a mystery, the origin of the viewings was scarcely less so. Gabriela would enter into no conversation at all during them, and although she would talk eagerly and intelligently on any other subject at any other time, she would never allow even the most oblique reference to them.

That is, again, not quite accurate. I doubt if she had ever needed actually to refuse to discuss them. She gave the impression that she would not do so, and I can imagine no one in our circle having the courage, stupidity or bad taste to try.

A similar restraint was evident at the viewings themselves. About fifteen of us, often almost as many women as men, sat around her as she showed us her strange illumination. Our arousal was not in question: erections began to strain at the men's elegant trousers even before the room was darkened, and the women's lips began to moisten and open. But the atmosphere was almost religious. Any move would have been sacrilege; unthinkable.

I was first invited to a session by a close friend. I later found that the same had happened to him, and no one seemed to know anyone who had found out about them in any other way. Yet Gabriela was still in her twenties, and the whole thing could only have been going for about ten years at the most. How had it started? Why did she do it? Had some former lover been involved? The fact that no money changed hands in these sessions, not even in the most indirect fashion, so that she obtained no benefit beyond the silent adoration of her audience, made them still more mysterious.

In all honesty, I would allow myself to speculate like this only at rare intervals. The sessions themselves were a sufficient obsession for all of us, I suspect; and while she permitted us to sit silently staring at her glowing genitalia, our excitement mounting during the ten minutes that she allowed, why should we worry about motives or origins?

My reference to a lover was, in any case, misleading. We all loved Gabriela, as a lively talkative companion and as a semi-religious object, but none of us had made love to her, as far as any of us knew. It was assumed, for reasons that were always unclear, that she was a virgin. Perhaps to some extent this was a face-saver for us, but we believed in its literal physical truth. Her social appearances were always solitary, one of the crowd but never with any one person, and the sessions took place at her flat, where there was no sign of any inhabitant other than herself and her cat. Afterwards we all left in couples or larger groups, leaving Gabriela alone. Perhaps she was as much aroused as we were as we hurried to the consummation of the desires awoken by the sight of her.

I have tried to imagine her masturbating afterwards, her fingers a dark shadow against that perfect pink light, but I have never found the image entirely convincing. In the sessions she showed no sign of any reaction to our gaze or to her own exposure; neither fear nor pleasure. None, that is, until the night of Eduardo's visit.

I had known Eduardo for about six months, since he had moved to our head office from a small branch. Both his skills and his personality had soon outgrown the provincial district's limitations, and I had been the one responsible for recognising his talent, nurturing it and arranging his move. To some extent he was still my protégé, although the need for any further help from me had almost disappeared.

Inviting him to Gabriela's was the ultimate sign of my trust and regard for him, and I did it only because I had complete faith in his discretion and his ability to gain pleasure from such a special experience. I have been blamed since, naturally, but the end result was so unexpected yet, after what happened, so inevitable that I cannot accept that blame is appropriate.

The session began normally. Gabriela gave us drinks, acknowledged old and new faces, and showed no more than normal politeness towards Eduardo. We took our places. The room was darkened, and Gabriela started to raise her skirt. At first, in the complete darkness, only the rustling of the material told us this, but as the rising hemline cleared her knickers they became visible from within. The light shining through their thin silk gave them a deep pink radiance as if a colour slide of her cunt were being projected onto them from underneath. They were slipped down, passing into the darkness again as her luminous pudenda were exposed.

At this point there was always a little sound from the spectators which emphasised the silence rather than breaking it, a sort of genteel half-gasp, almost imagined rather than heard. It seemed slightly louder to me this time, and I thought the increased volume came from Eduardo's contribution, but this could be retrospective imagination at work. What was certain was that he was aroused by the sight. This in itself was not, of course, surprising: what was surprising, though it took a while for me to understand this, was the fact that I could *tell.* His excitement had become obvious in the darkness because of the pink glow lighting up his bulging trousers.

There were some real gasps around us now, and one of them came from Gabriela. I heard movement, saw her glowing cunt change position as if she had begun to crawl across the carpet towards us. Then I saw her hand outlined against Eduardo's flies as she tugged at his zip. His prick, illuminated in exactly the same way as her cunt, sprang out from its captivity into a new prison in Gabriela's mouth.

It wasn't held there for long. After showering it with kisses she realigned herself so that their two shining organs coincided, and they began to fuck passionately, their genitals now only intermittently visible as they writhed and bounced together. It was all over very quickly, that bizarre and rather beautiful sex show, and soon after they had both reached orgasm someone switched on the lights.

Our feelings as spectators were rather mixed. Most of us had been too shaken by the unprecedented nature of the event to be properly aroused by it, and, though the implications were still unclear, I think we all sensed a threat to the viewings.

As it happened, that *was* the last session, though not for the obvious reason. Gabriela and Eduardo became, instantly it seemed, a happy and loving couple, and are still together. There was no opposition from either of them to the notion of continuing the sessions as a double exhibition, allowing us to share that beautiful, illuminated lovemaking. But at the climax of that first coupling, sadly, mysteriously, somehow inevitably, both lights had gone out.

The Circle

J.P. Kansas

I arrived at the address Marcie had given me at ten minutes before nine. The midtown neighbourhood was mostly older offices and loft buildings. I paid the cheerfully psychotic taxi driver and got out of the cab. At this hour, the street-level stores were all covered with heavy metal gates. The street was dark and deserted.

I was nervous. I had spoken to Marcie only once, on the telephone. She had sounded intelligent, but the low fidelity of the phone had removed all distinctiveness from her voice, as it usually does to women's voices. It had been a quick, strange conversation. "I don't like bars. There's a club I like to go to. We could meet there if you like," she had said.

"What kind of club?" I had asked.

"They have entertainment."

"What kind of entertainment?"

"Erotic entertainment."

I had swallowed, and I had felt the tips of my ears grow hot. From our mutual friend's all-too-brief description, Marcie was at least ten years younger than I was, but I had felt like an adolescent: excited and embarrassed all at once. In the last years of my failing marriage, and in the eighteen months since its demise, I had been to several places that offered erotic entertainment — mostly topless bars, but a few places that featured total nudity, and one place that presented actual sexual acts on stage — live, as they put it. It would never have occurred to me, though, to suggest that I meet a woman at such a place. It was totally unimaginable that a woman would suggest it to me.

Our mutual friend had suggested that Marcie was too sophisticated for me, and perhaps he was right. But I was eager to find out what that meant. "Sure, if that's what you'd like," I had replied. We quickly made arrangements and got off the phone.

The address turned out to be a pre-war building in the middle of the block, with an elaborate stone facade that had been modernised with a lot of chrome and glass at street level. The front door was locked, but there was a modern buzzer system. The button for suite 901 was unlabeled. It responded immediately when I rang it.

The lobby was very narrow, but beautifully tiled in marble and granite. The directory had no listing for suite 901. The call buttons for the elevator were of the modern, vandal-proof kind: shallow metal domes that blended almost seamlessly into the surrounding plate. The elevator was already on the ground floor and opened immediately. It was similarly modern and featureless.

The elevator door opened on the ninth floor, and I stepped out into a small vestibule surrounded by glass. In front of me were heavy glass doors, beyond which was a small reception area. It looked more like a dentist's office than an emporium of erotic entertainment.

An attractive dark-haired woman in a crisp, white outfit faced me at a desk behind a partition. She must have pressed a button at her desk because I heard a buzzing sound at the door. I pushed the door open and walked into the reception area, which was carpeted but very plainly decorated. There were two couches but no table, no magazines, not even a piece of artwork on the bare white walls.

"Hello," said the receptionist, smiling professionally. I was again reminded of a dentist's office.

"Hi," I said, dropping my briefcase at my feet.

"I'm meeting Marcie."

"You must be Jim, then." I nodded. "She's already inside. You can hang up your coat and put your briefcase away. It'll be perfectly safe."

I nodded and turned to hang up my coat and stow my case in the area next to her desk. There were twenty or so hangers, only about half of which were being used.

"Before you go inside, please familiarise yourself with this," the receptionist said, offering me a small card laminated in plastic.

I took it and sat down, puzzled, on one of the couches, and read the card:

Rules of the Circle
1. No touching others.
2. No talking.
3. No leaving your chair except to leave the circle.

Each seating lasts forty-five minutes, beginning on the hour. One bell marks the start of the seating. Two bells are rung, five minutes Before the end, and three bells are rung, at the end. At the three bells, you should be prepared to leave the circle, but please wait until the attendant turns your chair to face away from the circle. Then leave quickly and silently.

As I puzzled over the card, I heard the receptionist buzz another guest in. A young man entered who might have worked for the same law firm I did. He carried a similar briefcase, wore a similar raincoat, and, I saw after he hung up the raincoat, a similar dark blue suit, white shirt, and conservative tie. Unlike me, his hair was blonde, and he wore glasses. The young man greeted the receptionist, took out his wallet, and counted out some money. I did not see how much it was, but it seemed to involve twenties and tens.

"Thank you," said the receptionist. "You can go right in." The young man disappeared down a corridor to the right.

I got up and handed the receptionist the card with the rules. "How much is it?"

"It's been taken care of for tonight."

I raised my eyebrows. "And how much is it regularly?"

"A hundred dollars to join the circle, and then fifty dollars each sitting."

I raised my eyebrows again but said nothing.

"You can go right in. Just give the attendant your name and she'll show you to your seat."

I walked down a long, brightly lit corridor, past a men's room and a ladies' room and turned a corner. Suddenly I faced a door with a sign saying, 'The Circle'.

I opened the door, which gave on to a large, dark, high-ceilinged, windowless room. About twenty feet from where I stood, a dozen or so chairs were arranged in a circle. All but one of the chairs were faced into the circle. The chairs seemed to be occupied; women's handbags hung from some of the hooks attached to the chair backs. Looking between the chairs, I caught glimpses of some of the occupants. Spotlights suspended from the ceiling cast a bright, warm light on the occupants of the circle but left the rest of the room in shadow.

I stepped towards the chairs. Out of the surrounding darkness, a young woman in a white outfit approached me. She had dark eyes and dark hair. She was very pretty, with an intelligent smile. She stopped and stood before me, seeming to be waiting for me to speak.

"I'm Jim," I said, smiling awkwardly.

"Yes," she murmured, almost whispering. "You're the last one for this sitting. Come with me. Chair number six." She gestured towards the unoccupied chair that faced away from the circle. I sat down, resting my arms on the thin, padded rests. "Enjoy yourself," she said softly as she grasped the back of my chair and, with some effort, rotated it to face the circle. The chair seemed to lock into place.

As I had thought, the circle consisted of twelve chairs. With my arrival, all the chairs were occupied.

I looked at the others in the circle.

If I was seated in chair number six, the man who had come in to the reception area just after me was seated opposite me, in chair twelve. He was just taking off his suit jacket, and turned around to reach behind himself, apparently to hang up his jacket.

To the right of the young man, in chair one, was a woman who looked to be in her mid twenties. She had shoulder-length straight blonde hair parted in the middle, blue eyes, and a smooth white complexion. She wore a white silk blouse buttoned to the neck and the sort of long, pleated plaid skirt I associated with Catholic school, dark brown penny loafers, and navy blue knee socks. As she saw me looking at her, she smiled slightly, and nodded. Was she Marcie? I regretted not getting a description from our mutual friend. I didn't even know the colour of Marcie's hair.

In chair two was a tall, lanky man of about my age, thirty-five, with straight black hair and a heavy black moustache. He wore a colourful flannel shirt that was open at the neck, blue jeans, and low brown boots. He smiled at me speculatively when he noticed me looking at him, and I turned away abruptly.

In chair three was a woman of perhaps thirty years old, with luxuriantly long red hair. She wore a heavy black turtleneck sweater and a loose-fitting black skirt. Her eyes were hidden by large, dark sun glasses. She, too, might be the woman who had invited me to this place.

In chair four was a strikingly good-looking man with dark eyes and generous dark hair. My view of him was partially blocked by the next chair, but I could see that he wore an expensive-looking pink shirt and well-tailored dark slacks.

Immediately to my right, in chair five, was a somewhat younger woman with sharp features and intense green eyes, dressed like a professional of some kind, in a bulky sweater and a long gray pleated skirt. She smiled at me as I turned to look at her. Her smile was so warm and open that I thought she, too, might be the woman I was to meet.

To my left, in chair seven, was a woman about my own age with a sweet, round face and tightly curly black hair. She wore a flannel shirt and a jumper of faded denim. She met my eyes quizzically, with a teasing look in her eyes. There was no way for me to decide whether she was Marcie, either.

In chair eight was a man in his fifties or so, with gray hair and a full gray beard. He wore a tan sweater and faded jeans.

In chair nine was a beautiful Japanese woman with long,

black hair. She wore red lipstick and her eyes were dark with mascara and eyeliner. She wore a tight-fitting red sweater and a short, tight red leather skirt with a zipper running up one side. On her feet were high-heeled red shoes.

In chair ten was a small, delicate-looking young man in his early twenties, clean-shaven, with light blonde hair. He wore a Hawaiian shirt and light-coloured slacks.

Lastly, in chair eleven was a tough-looking woman with very short, dark hair. She wore not only a half-dozen earrings and ear cuffs, but had a thin gold ring in her nostril. She wore a leather vest over a denim shirt, tight leather shorts, and high-heeled leather boots. I doubted that she was Marcie: she looked as if she preferred women to men. But I had noticed that she had been observing me since I had sat down, and as I met her eyes she nodded at me familiarly, as if she already knew me, which made me uncertain.

It had taken only a few moments for me to look over the others in the circle, and for them to look me over. As we continued to look at each other, waiting for whatever was to begin, I was aware of the woman in the white outfit, walking outside of the circle of light, stopping behind one chair or another, watching us.

I heard a single bell sound, distinctly but not obtrusively. In response to the bell, the atmosphere in the circle seemed to change. People rearranged themselves, moving their hands from one position to another. Some of the members of the circle met my eyes, smiling slightly, some seeming almost about to speak. There was an expectancy, an excitement, as just before the curtain rises at the theatre, or before a thunderstorm.

I feel colossally stupid to admit this, but at first I wondered what the entertainment would be, what sort of erotic performer would appear in the centre of the circle. I tried to look beyond the circle, over the backs of the chairs and between them, to see if anyone was coming, but all I saw was the attendant.

When I brought my eyes back to the circle, I suddenly realised that we were going to be our own erotic entertainment, although I had, as yet, no real evidence of this. People were barely moving at all. The red-haired woman at three o'clock had one hand resting on her stomach just below her breasts, the fingertips moving lightly back and forth. The man I supposed was a lawyer opposite me had a hand on his thigh just below the knee, rhythmically squeezing. The woman at one o clock I had decided had gone to Catholic school was simply toying with the top button of her blouse. The man at ten o'clock in the Hawaiian shirt had each hand under the opposite armpit, gently squeezing the muscles of his chest. The woman in leather at eleven had both hands between her thighs, but she was not moving them at all. No, none of them was doing anything that would have called attention to itself had it been done, for example, in a dentist's waiting room.

How did I know, at that moment, with absolute certainty, what was to unfold? It was in their faces. Everyone was watching everyone else, meeting each other's eyes – except, of course, for the woman in the sunglasses – smiling, teasing, daring. It seemed to be a game. Who was going to begin? Who was to go further than the others had already gone?

In that moment when I first realised what was going to happen, I experienced a tumultuous confusion of impulses and feelings. I felt scalded with embarrassment and a feeling of almost ridiculous naïveté that I had not understood sooner. I felt an irresistible desire to leap from my chair and run away, and I felt paralysed. I felt almost sickened with fear, and I felt almost painfully excited. I know I was blushing and trembling, and my hands were squeezing the ends of the armrests of my chair. I felt cold, and my face felt hot. I felt as frightened and excited as when I was just ten years old, and the girl my age next door had pulled down her pants and let me take a look at her bottom.

There was still nothing actually to see, but inside my clothing I was uncomfortably hard. Without removing my hands from the armrests, I tried to shift my position in my seat, to manoeuvre my erection into a more comfortable and less obvious position, but without success. My eyes jumped from one person to the next, as fascinated by their faces as by their hands. Several of the women, as their eyes danced around the circle, seemed to have looked at my crotch, with its unmistakable advertisement of my excitement. Which of them was Marcie? Which one had invited me to this? What would she think of me if I just sat there and didn't participate? What would she think of me if I did? What did I think of a woman who came to such a place? What did I think of a woman who would invite me there? What would we say to each other afterwards? What would we do?

I had no answers for any of these questions. My mouth was filled with saliva, but it felt strangely dry.

As I sat there, frozen, my hands gripping the armrests as if I were a passenger in an airplane about to crash, unable to decide whether I was in an erotic dream or an erotic nightmare, the others in the circle moved with a tantalising and agonising gradualness. Although my mind was filled with a crazed jumble of anticipatory erotic imaginings, in reality nothing much had happened yet. The woman in the three o'clock chair I had mentally dubbed the Catholic had unbuttoned the top button of her blouse and was lightly caressing her neck. The woman in leather at eleven o'clock whom I had decided was a lesbian had put the tips of her fingers into the waist of her leather shorts. She smiled at me as she noticed me looking at her. I smiled back in embarrassment.

I felt like an idiot, like a cat confused by too many birds, as I turned my head back and forth to look from person to person, or at least from woman to woman.

The red-haired woman in sunglasses at three o'clock had slipped her hands under her turtleneck sweater, but they seemed to be doing nothing more than resting on her stomach. The Japanese woman at nine o'clock was stroking her thigh where her skirt ended. To my left, the curly-haired woman in the seven o'clock chair had put her hands under the panel of her jumper. To my right, the green-eyed woman had simply intertwined her fingers and rested her hands just below her breasts.

Although I did not really want to see what the other men were doing, it was unavoidable. The lawyer at twelve o'clock had taken off his tie and had unbuttoned the top button of his shirt, and had one hand in his pants pocket near his crotch. The Hawaiian shirt at ten had also unbuttoned his shirt, and was stroking the base of his throat. The other men also had their hands in their pants pockets or at their chests.

Things progressed with a delicious, agonising slowness. At first I caught no more than peeks of brassieres or panties. On the women, buttons were unbuttoned and fasteners were unfastened, but clothes were not removed. On the men, belts were loosened and flies unzipped, but nothing more. On both men and women, the clothing slipped down or parted as if of its own will, a little at a time, revealing at first only glimpses of bare skin. But like a summer sprinkle that eventually gets everyone wet, little by little the men and women in the circle were revealing themselves. The cups of the Catholic woman's brassiere had moved lower and lower under her hands until, with a start, I realised that her breasts were completely bare, the nipples provocatively swollen and hard. I suddenly imagined rising from my chair and crossing the circle to suck on them, and my mouth filled with saliva. I shyly glanced up to meet her eyes. She looked at me with an expression I could not decipher — challenging? disappointed? hurt? Embarrassed, I looked away, and suddenly realised that all the other men — except me — and almost all the women were also entirely or nearly bare-chested.

Like most men, I had seen thousands if not tens of thousands of women's breasts, in men's magazines and in erotic videos and mainstream movies. In real life, I had seen the breasts of perhaps a few dozen women, including girlfriends, my wife, and the erotic performers in topless bars and elsewhere. And, like every heterosexual man I knew, I found the sight of an attractive woman's breasts endlessly and inexplicably novel and fascinating and delightful and arousing. But little if anything in my past compared to the experience of sitting in a room with six bare-breasted women one of whom I was on a sort of date with. My head felt heavy and light at the same time, and my mind felt dulled and sleepy. I wanted to close my eyes, but I could not help but look hungrily from one woman to the next.

I gripped the armrests more tightly than ever, dizzy with arousal, unable to move except for my head and eyes. I was greedy to see everything at once. I noticed that the lesbian at eleven o'clock had a gold ring in her left nipple, and was toying with it. I shivered and looked away.

The woman in the chair to my right was caressing her wonderfully full breasts with both hands, squeezing them and then passing her palms over her large, dark nipples. I swallowed, almost choking on my own saliva.

She turned her head and raked her eyes down my body with a disappointed, quizzical expression. Shamed, I took my eyes away.

Across the circle, the Catholic woman was rolling the nipples between her thumb and forefinger. Her breasts were small and delicate, like just-ripened fruit.

Everywhere I looked, the women were touching their breasts. Of course, I had seen women caressing themselves before, too. In pornographic films, it was commonplace. In the topless bars, the women commonly pretended to arouse themselves, and the live sex acts I had seen often involved women caressing themselves to real or simulated orgasm. All of those sights were exciting, but being there in the circle was far more arousing, almost unbearably so. The fact that the people in the circle were apparently not paid performers, but ordinary people, like myself, made it astonishingly intimate and revealing. And although I had not touched myself, I was on the brink of orgasm.

Sitting and staring, I suddenly remembered when I was an early teenager and, alone in the house, had discovered my older brother's collection of men's magazines. If I had ever seen such photographs before, they had frightened and repulsed me, and I had done my best to pretend to forget about them. Since the last time I had seen them, though, I had discovered masturbation, and this changed everything. Suddenly, the explicit and revealing photographs had an almost dangerous power. Lightheaded, my hands shaking and my heart pounding, my penis trapped awkwardly in my clothing, I paged frantically through the photographs of the pretty young women displaying and caressing themselves. I still remember the photograph that shocked me into ejaculating in my pants: a curly-haired young woman sitting against a pile of pillows on a bed, smiling coyly at the camera, her knees up and spread wide, her pelvis tilted forward, the forefinger of one hand on her clitoris, other forefinger at the mouth of her anus, almost but not quite touching. I remember sitting cross-legged on the floor of my brother's bedroom, holding the magazine before myself with both hands, staring at that young woman and her tantalising promise of taboos to be broken, as shocked by the force of my own orgasm as by that photograph.

It was just that sort of astonishment that I felt as I sat in the circle, and I felt almost as young and overwhelmed. I ached with a desire for orgasm and with a fear of reaching it. I could not imagine the embarrassment of ejaculating into my underwear, as I had done as a teenager that afternoon, and yet I could imagine it vividly. Briefly, I again imagined getting up and leaving the circle, but I feared that the very act of standing would cause my penis to rub against my clothing and send me into orgasm. I was now even more paralysed.

Even as my mind juggled these memories and thoughts, my eyes raced frantically around the room, with giddy exultation consuming everything the women were doing, and with uncomfortable fascination observing everything the men were doing. Hands were now very definitely on genitals, but — if this is possible to imagine under such circumstances — discreetly. The men's pants, although opened, were still at their waists, and their hands in their pants. All but one of the women were wearing skirts of one sort or another, and had one hand at their breasts and one slipped under their skirts. The one exception, the lesbian in chair eleven, had, like the men, loosened her fly and had her hand in her pants.

Like a swimmer who had stayed underwater too long, I inhaled suddenly and deeply, and realised that the atmosphere of the circle had filled with the intoxicating musky odours of sexual excitation. I realised also that the room was alive with the sounds of arousal. To my left, the curly-haired woman was sighing softly, and to my right I heard the wet sound of a mouth on skin. Turning, I caught sight of the green-eyed woman holding her breast to her mouth, licking and sucking her own nipple. Out of the corner of her eye, she saw me looking at her, and she turned and, smiling, stuck her tongue at me. Swallowing hard, I turned my head away for what seemed like the hundredth time that evening.

Opposite me, the man who had started out so conservatively dressed was now considerably less so. His tie and shirt were both off, and his suit pants were at his ankles. He was pinching his nipple with one hand, and with the other rubbing himself through his tight-fitting bikini underpants.

The Japanese woman had removed her skirt, and was rhythmically pulling the fabric of her underpants between her labia as her hand danced lightly over her breasts.

To my left, I heard a distinctive rhythmic sound and turned my head to see that the man in the Hawaiian shirt was the first to reveal himself completely. His pants and underwear at his knees, he held his scrotum with his left hand as he encircled his penis with the thumb and forefinger of his right hand and moved them up and down, drawing the loose flesh with them.

Except in erotic videos and in the few live erotic performances I had seen, I had never seen another man's erect penis. In truth, I found other men's penises, whether erect or flaccid, faintly repulsive, and preferred my erotic entertainment to consist of women alone or with each other. Now, I was both fascinated and repelled as he lazily moved his fist up and down the long shaft. I brought my eyes up to his face. He was smiling seductively at someone across the circle, perhaps the tall man with the moustache at two o'clock.

Now, one after another, the members of the circle were following the lead of the man in the Hawaiian shirt. I heard a shift of weight to my left, and turned to see the curly-haired woman in the seven o'clock chair, who when I had last looked was wearing only a pair of white cotton bikini underwear, raise her hips and tug them off to reveal a thick black jungle of pubic hair.

Across the circle, the Catholic, her hands still on her breasts, lifted her legs and let her skirt drop down her thighs. As she spread her legs, I saw that she wore no underpants, and was completely clean-shaven. As my eyes leaped from her crotch to her face, I saw that she had been enjoying my reaction. She smiled at me as she brought both hands down her body to her vulva, and I looked away again, feeling absurdly embarrassed by my own embarrassment. Next to her, the lawyer pulled aside his bikini briefs and brought out his penis, its tip glistening with fluid. Next to him, the lesbian put her booted feet at the edge of her seat and pulled her shorts down over them. As she let her shorts drop to the floor and parted her knees, I saw that she had a ring in one of her labia. The sight was so unexpected and so surprising I felt a small spark in my groin, almost but not quite igniting the wet fire of my orgasm.

Everyone but me had now uncovered their genitals and was masturbating openly. Five men stroked their penises with one or both hands to the same even, deliberate rhythm, some staring at the women, some meeting the eyes of other men, some looking at both. The six women were caressing themselves at a more varied rhythm, their styles also more varied. The Catholic had turned on one hip and brought her legs up. She was using the forefinger of one hand to stroke the side of her clitoris up and down, from the front, while the other hand was at her vagina, from behind. The red-haired woman in sunglasses at two o'clock had her legs thrown over the sides of her chair, spreading herself very wide. She seemed to have two or three fingers covering her clitoris, which she moved in a rapid, circular motion. The woman to my right held a small silver phallus in her left hand, pressing it into herself rhythmically as she used her right hand to hold her breast to her mouth. The curly-haired woman to my left was using the flat of her right palm in a rocking rhythm on her pubic mound as she squeezed her right breast with her left hand. The Japanese woman at nine o'clock had both hands at her crotch, although I could not see what she was doing with them. And the lesbian at eleven seemed to have the middle finger of her left hand inside her vagina as she ran the middle finger of her right up and down between her labia.

A movement to my right caught my eye, and I turned my head to see that the man in the two o'clock chair, staring apparently at the man in the Hawaiian shirt, lifted his left hand, in a fist with the thumb extended, to his mouth. He opened his lips and put his thumb in his mouth, unmistakably miming fellatio.

To my left, I heard a loud groan, and turned my head again. It was the man in the Hawaiian shirt. His semen spurted from his penis and over his fist as his body jerked spasmodically.

Even before he had finished ejaculating, the attendant stepped between his chair and the chair at eleven o'clock. The attendant, wearing what appeared to be surgical gloves and looking remarkably composed, was holding a box of tissues in one hand and what I assumed was a waste receptacle in the other. As soon as the man had wrung the last droplet of pleasure from his penis, he took a few tissues and began to wipe himself off.

To my right, I heard another moan. I turned my head and

saw that the green-eyed woman had both hands between her legs now, moving them quickly. She was staring across the circle, and was obviously close to her own orgasm.

I looked across to see what she was staring at, but I could not tell for certain. The lawyer was completely naked except for his conservative black socks. One hand cupped his scrotum as the other went up and down his shaft, which seemed to be completely wet with saliva or pre-ejaculatory fluid or both.

The Catholic, still turned on one hip, was still running the middle fingers of both hands between her legs, one from the front and one from the back. From the front, she used her right hand to part her labia. I watched as she inserted the middle finger of her left hand into her vagina, draw it out, move it backward, and insert it into her anus.

Shocked and thrilled by this sight, I felt my orgasm burst out of my testicles and through my penis, quick and hot. I heard myself cry out loudly, sounding even to myself like an animal in pain. My pleasure so intense it was like anguish, I felt my semen spreading rapidly between my penis and my groin as my body clenched again and again and my hips thrust forward.

As my pleasure faded, I looked down, immediately worried about the effect my semen would have on my clothes, imagining the shame of going home with a dark, circular stain at my crotch. Abruptly I became aware that the attendant had stopped to my left, offering the tissues.

My modesty suddenly seemed absurd. Quickly, I pulled my shirttails out of my waist, unfastened my pants and pulled them down to my ankles, and then somewhat more deliberately took my underpants down my thighs. I took a few tissues from the box the attendant offered and wiped up the semen, most of which lay between my groin and the shaft of my penis. I used another tissue to make sure that the inside of my underpants was dry, an I then threw all the tissues into the receptacle the attendant held toward me.

Called elsewhere in the circle by the moans of another man reaching orgasm, she stepped away. I sat for a moment, oddly content and relaxed, no longer embarrassed or ashamed, my penis still erect and twitching, one hand at its base. All around me, others in the circle continued to masturbate, their moans and sighs unrestrained.

Distinctly, over these sounds, came two bells: five minutes before the end of the sitting. To my right, the green-eyed woman shrieked, lifting her buttocks entirely off her chair, her hands moving the silver phallus in and out of herself faster than seemed possible.

It was suddenly as if I had not reached orgasm at all. My testicles ached with a leaden fullness, and my penis was taut and heavy. Without hesitation, I encircled it with my fist and began to move my hand in that well-practised rhythm. I looked across the circle. The Catholic, her fingers moving rapidly in and out of both orifices, met my eyes and smiled. Her smile seemed to radiate directly into my groin. For the first time, I felt no need — in fact, no ability — to take my eyes in search of another, more compelling sight. Like an apple tree in a violent autumn wind, the circle was yielding its fruit all at once.

I could no longer distinguish the source of each sound of pleasure, and it didn't matter. We were all feeling the same pleasure together. I felt a strange sense of kinship — no, of love — for everyone in the circle, even the men, whose eyes I had been so carefully avoiding. With our eyes still locked on each other's, the Catholic and I reached orgasms at virtually the same time. Marcie? I mouthed silently, just before a frighteningly loud, guttural groan wrenched itself from me. My second orgasm was so intense it unsettled me, and I could not help but close my eyes.

With my eyes still closed, I heard three bells, and felt something light drop on to my crotch. I opened my eyes to see that the attendant had given me a few more tissues, although my second orgasm had produced so little fluid I needed only one. Wiping myself up, I looked across the circle at the Catholic, who, like the others in the circle, was busy rearranging her clothing and did not look up. Crumpling up the tissues, I looked around for the attendant. She was standing behind the nine o'clock chair. The Japanese woman was apparently already dressed and ready to leave. With a tug, the attendant unlocked the chair from its position facing into the circle and spun it around to face away. The Japanese woman got up, murmured something to the attendant, and disappeared from the light.

Keeping the tissues crumpled in my fist, I pulled up my underpants and slacks and put my clothing back in order. The attendant went from chair to chair as the members of the circle finished getting themselves ready to leave. She waited several seconds before going from one chair to the next, so that each participant did not get up to leave until the previous one had gone. Everyone seemed reserved and withdrawn now, and as far as I could tell no one was making eye contact with anyone else. The woman in chair one, whom I had decided was the one who had invited me there, waited for the attendant with her eyes downcast and her hands folded in her lap. When her turn came she did not look up, and she left without even glancing back toward the circle.

One by one, the others left the circle, until there was only the lawyer at twelve o'clock, now fully dressed and composed again, and me. Perhaps, I decided, the attendant was having us leave in the same order that we had arrived. As if in confirmation, the attendant went to the man opposite me, releasing his chair and turning it around. I listened to the sound of his shoes on the wooden floor until he went through the door.

The attendant circled the chairs. I sensed that she was standing behind mine, and I felt her tug it unlocked and turn it around.

"So. How'd you like it?" she asked softly, with a slight smile. Her face seemed a little moist and flushed, as if she had not been entirely unaffected by what had just happened.

"I don't know what to say. It was probably the most intense sexual experience I've ever had, and the strangest."

"Yes. I thought you might like it."

I looked up at her, puzzled and confused.

"I'm Marcie," she said, smiling playfully.

The Art Collection

Rosa Dolittle

They passed with relief through the heavy wooden door into the coolness of the museum. Paris was shimmering in the heat of August. The art collection, minor though it was, and housed in one of the less fashionable areas of the city where the narrow streets gave more shade, promised a welcome break from the melting boulevards and stifling cafés.

Absorbed in a thick, well-thumbed pulp novel, the receptionist barely looked at them as he gave them their tickets and change. It was evidently a quiet period, if this obscure place could be imagined ever busy. A large winding staircase swept up to the entrance to the exhibits. There the white-haired curator examined their tickets benignly, then returned to his newspaper. He could see at a glance that they were not likely to vandalise the *objets d'art*, although this same appraising glance covertly took in the shape of Eva's hips beneath her cotton dress as she moved away across the floor of the first collection room.

They seemed an ill-assorted pair. Adam was well into middle age but still with a jauntiness about his slender figure; his mouth was sensuous, the protruding lower lip giving him an air of determination. His skin was still soft, but the fine wrinkles in his face and on his hands suggested dried leaves. Eva was a good deal younger, possibly by twenty years or more. Her body was at the peak of physical development, neither fat nor thin but fleshy as a peach is fleshy — firm and full. Her eyes were bright with the same humour that played about her mouth.

They wandered casually around the first room, looking at the objects displayed there — mainly furniture — without much interest, taking more pleasure in the coolness of the room. Windows partially shaded by blinds stretched from floor to ceiling down one side, opening out on to a courtyard garden filled with shrubs and flowers. The room itself was decorated in the sumptuous manner of the eighteenth century with silk wallcoverings, cornices lined with gold and rich tapestries depicting vague and somewhat obscure scenes from a mythical past. Pictures of naked goddesses in ornate frames were interspersed with large mirrors.

The position of one of the paintings struck Adam as singular. It was hung at eye level, as were the other paintings, and depicted a demurely naked young woman standing by a pool, either just having disrobed or about to dress. In the foreground, facing desolately out of the painting, was an old man. His back was thus towards the woman as if reluctantly respecting her modesty. But what caused Adam to pause and look repeatedly both at and away from the picture was the fact that, hung on the wall directly opposite, was a large gilt-framed mirror that reflected the whole of the painting back to itself. An old man designed the layout of this room, Adam speculated, or at any rate someone who took pity on the old man in the painting. Doomed never to look directly at that rosy flesh, he was able by means of the mirror to feast his eyes upon it for the duration of the daylight hours.

A notice near the door requested visitors not to touch anything. Pausing to inspect the silk wallcoverings, Eva said: "Imagine having a bedroom hung with silk," and she ran her fingers lightly over the fabric, which felt slightly coarse to the touch. Adam's hand passed lightly over her breasts and down to her hips and loins. "Don't touch!" he commanded. They laughed and moved on into the second room.

The dense silence of the museum pressed upon them like that of an empty church. They whispered rather than talked and stifled their laughter. A second, aged curator ambled through from a further room on his way to the front entrance. They nodded and smiled at each other. Adam had a flash of desire to open Eva's dress and show the curator her breasts.

The curator's footsteps ceased and the sound of muffled conversation and coughing floated through from beyond the door. Apart from Eva and Adam the building was empty. Looking about her, Eva's eye lit on an oil painting entitled "The Ecstasy of St Theresa". The saint was on her knees, half-swooning, her face lifted in joyous recognition as a light from heaven pierced the clouds, her flowing raiment and her heart. Eva stood gazing at the painting as Adam moved from one object to another.

Finally he came over to see what she was looking at. "Ah!" He breathed the words into her neck. "The saint acknowledges her god and comes as she does so." His lips moved up her neck and sought her ear and he whispered again, "Who is your god?" Eva sank her head back on his shoulder, her breasts offering themselves to his hands. She made no reply. "Worship me!" He demanded fiercely, pulling her round to look at him. She stared straight into the eyes that raked her face. "I do," she said simply. His hands stroked her neck and he kissed her with gratitude.

She pulled away from him half reluctantly, afraid the curator might return, but as she tried to move on he pulled her back against him once again and lifted the front of her skirt, rubbing his hand lightly up and down over her cunt. He kissed her mouth wetly, his tongue probing towards the root of her tongue. Her body melted and sank in upon itself, then a great surge of desire rushed through her like fire and she thrust herself against him, holding herself so that he could take what he wanted. However, seeing her arousal, he took only enough to whet both his appetite and hers. He released her and they walked on into the third room.

Eva's body was hot and pulsating, her legs felt weak. His sudden attack, desired, sought for and encouraged, made her want to throw herself to the polished floor, legs open. She would pull him down with her and they would fuck like animals, snarling, squealing, biting. She would be wild, open, stripped of everything except pure lust. She would be naked with lechery. The curators would come running in to try and separate them as if they were two rutting dogs: "M'sieur! Madame! S'il vous plait!" The ancient curators would grab hold of her, their wizened fingers would pluck at her flesh, grope between her legs, feeling the moisture there... She passed beneath a rather derivative picture of naked Susannah being spied on by the greybeard Elders with barely a glance.

She smiled at her fantasy as she wandered through the third room. It was larger than the previous two, evidently a central point of the collection. There were statues and sculptures as well as pictures and furniture. "Perhaps it's a display room," said Adam. Eva laughed and ran her hand up his erection. "For the sculpture," he added, unfastening the buttons of her dress and pulling it open to reveal her breasts. Eva laughed again and pulled away from him, covering herself.

In the centre of the room was an enormous piece of sculpture in white marble with several figures twisted and entwined together, writhing in grotesque rococo poses. One of the female figures was hurled outward from the main group, her torso flung towards the viewer, naked breasts foremost. "She has breasts like yours," commented Adam. An iron railing discouraged touching and yet another notice instructed, "Do not touch."

Eva leaned over the rail and stroked the marble breasts; they were smooth and cold. Adam put his hand on the back of her neck and gently pushed her head nearer to the hard white points; his other hand teased her nipple through the printed cotton dress. "Suck it," he whispered. "Suck her breast." Eva allowed him to push her face gently against the cold curves. Her warm lips touched the statue's cold, lifeless nipple. She felt her sex engorge with hot blood, her breasts strained out under her cotton frock towards Adam's hand to be squeezed and rubbed. Her lips closed around the marble breast, sucking and nuzzling it, and she ran her tongue repeatedly round and over the cold stone nipple.

Still squeezing and pinching her warm, hard nipple, Adam stood back slightly to watch her suck. Her posture now echoed that of the statue, her body slung forward across the rail, and he pulled her breasts out of her dress to complete the resemblance. Her increasing excitement in turn excited him. Her red lips glistened against the now wet breast of the statue, and he imagined that her wet mouth was her wet cunt and was seized with an overwhelming desire to fuck her.

As he watched her, feeling his prick move against the light cotton of his trousers, he heard footsteps in the room beyond, the sharp *tap-tap-tap* of a woman's high heels and the more muffled thud of a man's shoes. He caught his breath, ready to alert Eva, but the footsteps ceased. Adam didn't want to end the scene and Eva was oblivious to the imminent approach of the other couple. She remained splayed across the iron rail with her legs parted, ostensibly to steady herself. Adam pulled up her frock and eased his fingers into her wet, swollen hole. She moaned softly as one hand, lined and veined with experience, fingered the whole length of her vagina, while the fingers of the other examined her mouth, running along her lips and probing inside them, feeling how the marble entered her mouth, how the marble filled her mouth. "Keep sucking," he whispered as the anonymous footsteps echoed through the rooms once more. *Tap-tap, tap-tap, tap-tap*, then a pause, then again, *tap-tap, tap-tap, thud thud thud.*

Eva was now aware of the footsteps but they excited rather than alarmed her. Adam continued to explore her body, loving her excitement and her daring. He longed for the strangers to appear and see them, see him with his hands on and inside this passionately excited and aroused woman, see him holding her against the statue, willingly doing his bidding. *Tap-tap-tap. Thud thud.*

Her hands were now running over as much of the statue as they could reach, clutching at this cold, hard figure that received her caresses with utter and helpless indifference. *Tap-tap, tap-tap.* Adam's prick entered her suddenly, easily and hard, but there was no sound in the room apart from the tiny liquid sucking sounds of her sex as his prick moved rapidly in and out of her cunt, her juices pouring generously in response to his thrusts.

The footsteps had now moved closer, were now in the second collection room. *Tap-tap-tap. Tap-tap.* The voices were louder and clearer now, and Adam caught the words "Ecstasy... Theresa... beautiful." His hands were gripping Eva's hips now, and he thrust desperately to bring them both to climax. The anonymous voices were too near to wait, the footsteps too near to care any more. *Tap-tap. Thud. Thud. Tap-tap.* He pressed Eva harder down across the railing and exploded inside her, holding her tightly, expelling the last of his pleasure as the footsteps approached the doorway. The owners of the feet would appear any second now and see them... Adam wanted these strangers to see them.

"In answer to your query, madame..." The old curator's voice boomed around the rooms, and the footsteps receded to the first collection room. *Tap-tap. Tap-tap.*

Adam and Eva slumped to the floor sweating and panting. Quick, murmured Eva, before they come back again. Adam sat with his back against the railing and she moved close to him. His eyes never left her face as she lay between his thighs, and he wound his legs around hers, pulling them open with his heels. He began to probe and explore her darkness once more, finding the place, the rhythm she loved, moving his bony, lined fingers remorselessly up and down the soft, wet jelly of her sex, to and fro, now hard, now soft. Stopping, watching her gasp silently please, don't stop, please. Building the rhythm slowly at first then faster, faster. Her eyes glazed and she stared up at him almost like one dead, her mouth open as if in adoration, but she was barely aware of anything except his fingers moving the labia apart, feeling her heat, her hole, her pulsing desire. Now her lips opened wider, drawing back tightly as she came, silently screaming, "Oh my God! Oh Christ! Oh my God!" He plunged his tongue again and again to the back of her open throat, piercing to the heart of her desire.

Camping Out

Rosie Blue

This time last year, I was in the depths of despair. My boyfriend had left me for another woman, my flat was in the process of being repossessed and, to top it all, I'd lost my job.

The final blow came when I received a letter from the finance company demanding payment in full for my camper van. Stupidly, I'd bought the camper on impulse. I'd had some harebrained idea of driving into the hills with Steve and his insatiable dick for wild weekends of lust. But, as I discovered, he'd been getting plenty of that elsewhere for quite some time.

I'd been relying on the camper for somewhere to live. But it seemed I was set to lose everything, camper and all. Something had to be done, and quickly.

I couldn't even find part-time work, let alone a proper job. My thoughts turned to setting up a business of my own — but doing what? Even if I had a good idea, with no capital I couldn't rent business premises or buy stock. Other than home typing work, which wouldn't even keep me in food, there was nothing I could do. My best friend, Sarah, suggested that I turn the camper into a mobile fish and chip shop. She was always full of bright ideas, and that one wasn't too bad. But I simply didn't have the money to buy the necessary equipment.

In an effort to cheer me up, Sarah dragged me down to the pub. "You may as well spend your last few quid on vodka," she said as we walked into the saloon bar.

Two good-looking young men were sitting at the bar giving us the eye, but I wasn't in the mood to be chatted up. It seemed that one of them had just bought an American car. He was trying to impress us by telling his friend, loudly, that it was his mobile knocking shop.

"That's it! I'll use the camper as a mobile knocking shop!" I told Sarah. She was horrified by my suggestion — so was I! But it gave me an incredible idea.

I spent all next day working on the camper. Without ruining the interior, I built a plywood partition, effectively dividing the camper into two. The rear door led to the smaller space, which was just large enough to stand in. The front section retained the seating area, table, cooker and sink. I still had all the comforts of home and, most importantly, access to the driving seat via the dividing curtains.

I drilled a two-inch hole in the centre of the partition and carefully smoothed it off with sandpaper. Stocking up with teabags, water and milk, I was ready — except for one thing. The bright pink envelope would catch anyone's eye. I slipped my carefully worded letter of introduction inside, and put it in my bag.

It was dusk when I set out. I drove to the pub, and left the camper in a secluded corner of the car park.

There they were, the two young men, sitting in their usual spot at the bar. They were so I busy chatting up the barmaid that they didn't notice me. I kept a low profile as I made my way to the far end of the bar and bought a drink.

Pulling the envelope from my bag, I finished my drink and made my move. Making sure they didn't see my face, I made a point of dropping the envelope at their feet as I left. I prayed that they'd pick it up and read it.

I'd only been in the camper for five minutes when the rear door opened. A rolled-up ten-pound note appeared through the hole, then a long, stiff penis pushed its way through. I had done the right thing! I was in business!

Taking the end between my fingers, I moved the loose skin back and forth over the hard knob, slowly at first so as to give maximum value for money. The skin was smooth and silky, and I wondered which of the men it belonged to.

Working faster as the shaft stiffened and began to throb, I felt decidedly randy. It had been some time since I'd had a man, and the feel of a beautiful, hard dick in my hand was beginning to drive me wild. But I kept calm and told myself not to mix pleasure with business.

It wasn't until the head bulged and throbbed that I realised I wasn't properly equipped. Suddenly a shower of semen exploded from the end, covering my arm, my skirt and the carpet!

To my disappointment, the dying member slowly retreated through the hole and the rear door closed. I was left alone to clean up the mess — but I'd earned ten pounds! Pleased with my efforts, I put the kettle on for tea.

I'd just switched on the radio to keep me company when another ten-pound note dropped to the floor. A miserable-looking slug-like thing appeared through the hole and hung sadly in front of me. The kettle was nowhere near boiling, so I had plenty of time to earn another tenner before taking a tea break.

The penis soon hardened and turned into a handsome specimen as I worked my hand quickly up and down the shaft. This must belong to the other young man, I thought, humming to the radio and keeping an eye on the kettle.

He was taking rather a long time to come, so despite my aching wrist I quickened my stroke. As the head began to pulsate, I grabbed the tea-towel, it was all I had. Unfortunately, he pumped out his semen with such force that I only managed to catch a few drops, and the carpet got its second soaking!

Twenty pounds the richer, I put my feet up and was about enjoy a nice cuppa when, to my surprise, yet another ten-pound note appeared. I gazed expectantly at the opening.

Suddenly a massive, jumbo-sausage-like penis came into view. It was so big that I was surprised the owner managed to fit it through the hole! I made a mental note to enlarge it to cater for all sizes. Before working on the wondrous specimen, I spread the tea-towel on the carpet and made another mental note to buy a plastic mat and several boxes of tissues.

Using both hands, I grasped my third expectant dick. I surmised that the owner was considerably older than the other two, not because of the sheer size of his penis but because the skin was wrinkled and pitted with age. It had obviously been around for some years — eighty-odd, by the look of it! But, I told myself, it doesn't matter. Eighteen or eighty, they're all dicks in need of my attentive hands.

Concentrating on the smooth head, I became aware of a wetness in my knickers. My aching clit needed attention, and I was in two minds as to whether to slip the thing inside my cunny or not. But, determined to stick to my original business plans, I decided to finished the job in hand. My clit would have to wait. Another mental note: buy myself a vibrator!

The penis throbbed and twitched and increased in size to such an extent that it completely filled the hole. When the explosion came, spurt after spurt of white liquid shot from the purple, bulging head. It flew through the air, landing on the table, the carpet, and, of course, all over me.

Some minutes passed before the massive member deflated enough for its owner to retrieve it. When the rear door closed, I collapsed onto the small sofa — thirty pounds the richer.

The next day I enlarged the hole and lined it with a piece of black velvet, just to add a touch of comfort. With a box of tissues on the table and a large plastic mat covering the carpet, I was ready for the night shift.

I took Sarah with me to the pub, and told her that I would buy her a drink 'after work'. The poor girl hadn't got a clue what I was talking about. She sat there firing questions at me until I drove into the car park, where she finally shut up. As we climbed into the back of the van, I told her to be patient and very quiet while we waited.

She was amazed when a ten-pound note dropped to the floor. And positively stunned when a hard, long dick appeared through the hole.

I didn't recognise the penis. "A new client," I whispered, grinning at Sarah. Open-mouthed, she sat there with her eyes on stalks.

While I worked on the shaft, I told Sarah about my new business venture, but she wasn't listening. Seeing her hungry eyes transfixed on the bulging dick, I thought it only fair to let her have a go. Eagerly grabbing it, she worked the skin back and forth over the tip until it started to bulge in her tiny hand.

She watched excitedly as the semen shot out and dribbled

over the back of her hand and down her wrist, and seemed disappointed when the penis withdrew and disappeared. "Don't worry, there'll be plenty more," I said consolingly, passing her a tissue.

As the rear door closed, we both burst out laughing. "I can't believe it!" she screeched, wiping her hand. '"How much money have you made?" I didn't have time to answer; the door had opened again.

The money dropped to the floor, and a tiny dick fell limply through the hole. Sarah beat me to it. Gripping the little thing in her hand, she fell to her knees and eagerly started work.

The smallest dick I'd ever seen suddenly grew to one of the biggest. Sarah couldn't believe her eyes as it blew up like a long sausage balloon. Working like a Trojan, she soon had the veins bulging. I stood waiting with the tissues again, but nothing happened.

Poor Sarah's hand was beginning to ache, and she asked me to take over. Without losing the rhythm I continued the job until, at long last, the semen came cascading out in great torrents. This time it landed all over Sarah, to her delight.

When the client had gone, we drove off and parked the camper a few streets away. As we walked back to the pub Sarah worked out that I could earn as much as seven hundred pounds a week without too much effort. All I needed was ten clients a day.

The two young men were sitting in their usual place at the bar when we arrived. Fortunately, there was a free table within earshot of them. As soon as we'd got our drinks and sat down to listen to their conversation, one of them left.

Within seconds, he came back. "It's gone," he said to his friend despondently.

"It'll come back, just be patient. Anyway, the others haven't arrived yet," came the reply.

I looked at Sarah. "Others? How many have they told? How many are they expecting?"

"Don't worry. I'll give you a hand — or *them* a hand!" she reassured me with a giggle.

Over the next half-hour they were joined by ten more excited men, all laughing and joking about who should go first. Sarah and I finished our drinks and left. We had work to do!

I'd expected a group of men with bulging trousers to be waiting in the car park, but there was no one in sight when we parked the camper in our usual spot. We didn't have to wait long, though. The first client opened the rear door as soon as I'd turned the engine off. The inevitable ten-pound note dropped to the floor, and then a wonderfully hard, thick penis materialised.

We decided to take it in turns. Sarah won the toss, and went first. Talk about premature ejaculation — the thing spurted spunk all over the place as soon as she touched it. And I didn't even have time to grab a tissue before it disappeared.

By the time the third dick was sticking proudly through the hole, Sarah was getting pretty excited. "This is all very well, but I wouldn't mind one of these specimens inside me," she whispered. I'd been thinking the same thing. But despite my aching clit and drenched knickers, I was more interested in the money.

Sarah's luck was in a couple of dicks later. Carefully tattooed in ballpoint pen on the foreskin of a huge penis was — 'ORAL'? She grabbed a pen from her bag and wrote '£25' on the swollen shaft. The thing disappeared through the hole. To Sarah's great delight, the money dropped to the floor and the penis reappeared, complete with rubber.

Sarah didn't waste a second. She had the entire length in her mouth and was frantically lunging her head back and forth before I knew what was going on. Suddenly she stopped. "May as well make the most of it. Guide it in, will you?" she asked, pulling down her panties and backing her wet cunny towards the rubber-clad member.

Staring in disbelief, I positioned the hard knob between her swollen flaps and watched it disappear inside her hole. Jerking her hips backwards and forwards, she brought herself to a massive climax and crumpled to the floor in obvious ecstasy.

Sarah was well and truly satisfied, and as the penis retreated through the hole I noticed that the rubber teat was full. Sarah had definitely done a good job.

For the next hour, I brought off one dick after another. Sarah was useless. She just sat there with her hands inside her wet knickers, bringing herself off.

We — or, rather, I — finished off all the dicks in time for last orders. With the camper safely parked around the corner, we strolled into the bar, where a lot of satisfied young men were talking eagerly about their experiences. We listened in, hoping to discover who had invested twenty-five pounds in my business venture. But whoever the lucky young man was, he wasn't telling.

Sarah kept the twenty-five pounds she'd earned. And I was delighted when I counted my takings: I'd made over a hundred pounds! That would bring me up to date with the payments on the camper.

As I'd expected, Sarah was eager for a part-time job with my new company. There was still a long way to go before caught up with my bills, so I could only offer her twenty per cent of the takings. Excitedly, she agreed.

The following evening found us in the car park once again. Word had obviously got round — we milked a good pint of semen in our first hour! Fat thin, long, short, young, old, roundheads, cavaliers – between us, we wanked the lot.

Towards the end of the evening, we were worn out and looking forward to a drink before the pub closed. As we were packing up, a note slipped through the hole. 'I know who you are. Do me for free or I'll expose you!' I'd been wondering when we'd get our first troublemaker.

A small, ugly dickling appeared before our eyes. Sarah looked at me and nodded. I started to work or the shaft, but I was determined to stop at the crucial moment. No one was going to get a good orgasm for free!

When the dick was almost ready to shoot its load, Sarah pushed my hand away and took over. As it fired its first spurt, she pulled the foreskin right back and poured a kettle of hot water over the throbbing knob! We fell about laughing as the thing disappeared, its owner yelling and dashing across the car park in agony.

In the pub, we bought our drinks and looked around for the culprit. "He should be easy enough to spot," laughed Sarah. Sure enough, sitting in the corner was a man clutching his trousers and grimacing with pain. Poor sod — the water hadn't been boiling but it must have been bloody hot.

I recognised the two-timing bastard straight away. "Hi, Steve," I called, walking towards him. "Your insatiable dick's still getting you into hot water, then?"

Ah, sweet revenge!

Four Play

Claire Sawyer

I looked at it. There it was in print. It didn't sound like me at all. In fact, as I read it, I couldn't believe that a week ago I had actually sat down and written it. As I pored over it for the umpteenth time, the post landed on the mat in the hall outside. Making a mental note to go and get it in a minute, I read it again.

'Twenty-eight year-old woman. Attractive, blonde, single. Smoker. Disillusioned with the men she has met on her return from North America, seeks excitement and stimulation. Reply box no. 4536.'

I had written it after Mark and I had split up. I'd met him at a Knightsbridge party shortly after my return from Canada, where I had been working as a graphic designer in a publishing house. He had been quite nice-looking, and although the sex had been well, let's say, straightish — we'd got on quite well. On that last evening, we were lying in bed having a cigarette after we'd finished making love. Then he told me that he was engaged to someone else.

Jesus. Why do guys do it? Why do they all have to lie and cheat? I went mad. I cried and screamed, and then I hit him so hard around the face that I sliced some skin off his ear with my watch, which still gives me a sense of satisfaction. He shot out of the flat. Why the fuck did he lie?

Anyway, that's when I wrote the ad. Compared with some of the others, mine looked pretty ordinary. But when I wrote it I didn't want the message shrouded in euphemism and quaint metaphors. At least it was direct. After I'd sent the ad in, I put it out of my mind; indeed, I genuinely forgot about it. I'd bought my copy of the magazine a couple of days earlier and hadn't got round to opening it. Then, this morning, I'd remembered. Almost nervously, I turned to the lonely hearts section, and there I was. Little old me reduced to a line and a half of print.

'Excitement and stimulation.' It sounded a bit strong, but what the hell? I didn't have to see anyone if I didn't want to.

I made myself some coffee and lit my first cigarette of the day. I decided I would kick it when I started getting laid regularly again. I inhaled a good lungful and immediately felt better. Then I remembered the post. I rushed into the hall, where I found about a dozen letters. Apart from a bill and a piece of junk which went straight into the bin, the rest were replies to the ad.

Like a schoolkid, I ripped them open one by one. Most were from S&M cranks. There was one from an amputee and another from a guy — at least, I think he was male — who wanted me to crap all over him. And there was one in a nicely hand-written envelope from which, when I opened it, a photograph fell out.

It was of a guy, around thirty-five, maybe even forty. Good-looking, actually. He was dark-haired with a few lines around his eyes, but he had a crinkly smile, which I liked. The letter was straight as well. He was thirty-five, a writer (a lot of guys think you'll fancy them if they say that), but at least he spelled properly and the letter was laid out nicely; so I was prepared to give him the benefit of the doubt. He had a West London address. He said he'd like to take me out to dinner. Could I ring him?

I spent most of the day plucking up the courage to phone him. A couple of times I even went as far as dialling his number before putting the phone down at the last minute. Eventually, fortified by a couple of large gins and a spliff, I caught him.

He was charm personified, and suggested we meet at a pub off the King's Road. Would I prefer French or Italian, because he'd like to book somewhere?

We met up the following evening. I found him in the pub, recognised him from his picture, went out again, walked up and down the street and then went back in again. I took another long look before walking up and tapping him on the shoulder. We had a couple of drinks and then walked to a lovely little French restaurant on the King's Road, where all the staff seemed to know him.

The meal was wonderful. He had published a couple of novels and he'd had a play done on TV. He was divorced and his wife lived in America with his two sons, whom he adored. He had the gift of listening as well as appearing interested, a gift most of the guys I'd known had not acquired.

I talked and talked. I told him about myself, my job and Mark. At one point, I had to stop myself as I found myself discussing the sexual shortcomings of our relationship.

He shared a taxi with me to my flat and didn't try to kiss me. This half-bothered and half-flattered me. Perhaps he didn't fancy me. Perhaps he thought I talked too much. Jesus, I was thinking like I had fifteen years ago. Stop it, girl. Then he asked if I was free on the following Friday, and I found myself inviting him round for a meal. I'm proud of my cooking and told him so. He smiled and said he'd be delighted to come.

I took the afternoon off work to prepare the dinner. I'd decided on watercress soup, then lamb roasted with rosemary and garlic and served with new potatoes and mangetouts. Fruit salad would do for dessert.

Then, I dressed for him. Me and him. I wore a short black skirt because it sets off my (natural) blonde hair and I have a good tan, and my legs are my best feature. I wore nothing else except some good shoes and a necklace, which felt good — slightly decadent, but good.

It was then that the phone rang. He was dreadfully apologetic, but his sons were flying in that night. He'd completely forgotten. Could we make it another night? I was crestfallen. The bastard. I really wanted to see him. Realising my disappointment, he suggested that perhaps they could meet him at my flat. They weren't due until ten. We could eat at least. Almost without thinking, I agreed. He apologised again and said he'd be round at eight.

He loved the soup. We washed the lamb down with some good Volnay he had brought with him, and I opened some Moët, which we drank with the fruit salad. As we talked and flirted and smiled and made eyes, I rolled a joint and we settled down — me on the sofa and him in a chair — and listened to some good Miles Davis.

The dope worked and I went off into a haze — a sexy, sensual dream. I felt warm and moist. He must have sensed it. He came over and sat next to me. I think my dress had ridden up and I felt his cool hand on my thigh.

Almost instinctively, I parted my legs slightly. He looked onto my eyes and then kissed me gently on the lips. He nibbled my ears, my throat and my eyes and then he teased my lips before I felt his tongue inside my mouth. He told me how beautiful I was and then he pulled down the straps of my dress and bent his head so that he could nibble my breasts, slowly and so, so deftly.

I held his head to me and then he lifted up my legs and placed them on the sofa. I felt my skirt ride higher and a delicious draught of anticipation as I heard him murmur appreciatively when he found that I was wearing no knickers. He touched me gently and then murmured again when he found how wet I was. Jesus what was he doing to me? I was on heat and, God, did I want him to fuck me. Then I felt his tongue, hot and insistent as it worked its way inside me.

Then he licked me and expertly took my clitoris between his teeth and started to suck. Slowly at first and then more persistently, he built up an even rhythm until I thought I would die. I thrust myself up to him, and kissed his mouth with my vulva — a wet and languorous kiss. I felt his finger probing my anus and then it was inside me.

God, I was about to come. "Please. Not yet," I begged. He picked me up and kissed me and I pointed helplessly towards the bedroom. He carried me, my dress around my waist, and placed me down on the bed. He removed my dress and then I leaned towards him and helped him take his clothes off. His body was lean and muscular and his cock was hard and ready.

He entered me straight away and I abandoned myself to him. Within what seemed like seconds I had come.

It was then that the bell went. I sat bolt upright, the sweet sensation of orgasm just a memory. "Don't worry," he said. "That'll be my sons. I'll put them in the other room."

He quickly put his shirt and trousers on and then he was gone, leaving me naked and stoned, his semen still coming out of me.

I felt pissed off. The evening was over before it had begun. Sulkily, I pulled the duvet over me and rolled another joint. I heard voices from the next room, and as I became more stoned I had the germ of an idea. When he came back he sat on the bed and apologised profusely. I snuggled up to him and told him what I had been thinking.

I don't know what I imagined he would say, but he simply smiled and left the room. Within two minutes he had returned with his sons.

They couldn't have been more than eighteen, and they both wore T-shirts and jeans. They resembled their father, but in different ways. One had black hair, the other blond, and they looked incredibly desirable.

My seducer produced a bottle of champagne and we drank, me modestly under the duvet with three men sitting next to me on the bed. I passed the joint to the dark son, who smiled and inhaled. Then the blond boy grinned, and suddenly we were all talking.

We drank and smoked, and then the atmosphere, which had been sensual and friendly, changed and was in danger of dissipating. There was an awkward silence. It was then that I decided to take control. I removed the duvet and told them that I wanted to fuck all of them. Mutely, they acquiesced. They removed their jeans and T-shirts and their underpants. All were big, although the blond was the biggest of the three. And all were erect.

I beckoned to the blond to come towards the bed. He

approached slowly, uncertainly, and, lying on my front, I took his balls in my hand. I watched his face while with the other hand I started to stroke his perineum and gently inserted a finger inside his anus. The effect was electric. Instantly his penis seemed to jump towards me, poised in readiness in front of my parted lips.

His glans glistened and, with my finger still inside him, I started to lick the underside of his penis. A glistening blob of clear fluid appeared at the tip, which I licked and drank. Then, after teasing him for an age, I went down on him, taking as much into my mouth as I could manage. God, he was enormous. I started to suck, and as I inserted one more finger inside him I saw his eyes close in ecstasy and felt his hands grip my hair. I moved my head up and down, sucking harder and faster.

I took him deeper and deeper inside my mouth as he pumped at me and I felt the heat rise in me again. He stiffened further and thrust into the back of my throat. He came in hot, salty jets, which I devoured greedily. I sucked and sucked, draining every last drop of him.

I withdrew from him and gestured to the dark-haired son to lie down on the bed. Meekly he complied. His cock was firm and stiff, and, facing him, I impaled myself on it. I rode him hard, the juices flowing from me. I was insatiable. I wanted every orifice filled. I beckoned to my seducer and guided him into my mouth. He slid in, and as I licked, caressed and sucked, out of the corner of my eye I saw my blond behind me, massively erect again, with nowhere to go.

I leaned towards him and raised my buttocks. I wiggled and writhed as I fucked his brother and sucked his father, and pointed to my arse.

He needed no encouragement. Instantly, he was inside me.

I can't describe the ecstasy as his cock slid deep into me, so tight and so hard. At first it was deliciously painful and then it was just sublime, as with all the strength of youth he buggered me to distraction.

In unison we all fucked. I remember it as if it were a ballet. I was transformed into another dimension where time and space stood still. And then, as my orgasm approached, I was back on earth again.

It felt as if I were exploding. My clitoris, vagina and bowels were all on fire as I started to come. And as I climaxed, I rode harder and harder. A dam began to burst within me and I clasped my seducer's arse and squeezed his balls hard as I pulled him further and further into my mouth.

I think all our orgasms came at the same time. My seducer's semen hit the back of my throat as the boy beneath me shuddered and thrust joyously, releasing his own juice inside me. And then, sadly, the blond behind me thrust for the last time. Never had I felt a man so deep inside me. His semen exploded in my very bowels as my own orgasm reached its crescendo and then, sadly but slowly, started to fade.

It was over. I collapsed on top of them and, in a sea of semen and my own juices, fell asleep.

I woke a few hours later to find my lovers asleep next to me. I was pleased, as I'd half-expected them to have left. Curiously, I felt no shame as I scrutinised their bodies. All three were beautiful in their own way. Slowly, slowly I reached out into the night and found my seducer's cock. As I stroked it lightly and it came to life, I reached for another one. As it stirred, I moistened my lips and went down.